The ultimate challenge

Judge Ooka picked up the sword. Seikei saw that the smooth, dark wood was polished to a high gloss. It seemed almost to glow, like a real sword. "I entrust you with this sword," said the judge. "Treat it well, and use it with wisdom."

Seikei took the sword in his hands. He was almost dizzy with joy. He wanted to swing it through the air to test it, but knew that was something a boy would do in play. He acted as a samurai would, and bowed low before the judge before slipping the sword through his belt. "I am ready," he said.

Judge Ooka smiled. "We shall see."

"With a sharply authentic voice and an adeptly plotted story that progresses from the haunting ghost legend to the dark, volatile world of a traveling kabuki show, this mystery builds with stirring intrigue and plays out to a most satisfying conclusion." —*Booklist*

◆"The Hooblers employ suspense, action, superstition, and mystery to entrance readers with this tale of 18th-century Japan and a boy's search for honor. . . . Full of adventure, offering a vivid portrait of Shogun-era Japan, this is a remarkable novel."
—*Kirkus Reviews*, pointer review

The *Ghost* in the *Tokaido Inn*

DOROTHY
and
THOMAS
HOOBLER

SCHOLASTIC INC.
New York Toronto London Auckland Sydney
Mexico City New Delhi Hong Kong Buenos Aires

ISBN 0-439-38802-3

12 11 10 9 8 7 6 5 4 3 2 1   2 3 4 5 6 7/0

Printed in the U.S.A.   40

First Scholastic printing, February 2002

To our daughter, Ellen

Contents

Preface

By one way of measuring time, it was the year 1735. In Japan, it was known as the twenty-sixth year of the reign of the Emperor Nakamikado. It was the age of the samurai, the hereditary warriors whose code required one's every action to be guided by loyalty, courage, and honor.

Japan had known peace for more than a century. In 1603, Ieyasu Tokugawa had defeated the last of his rivals in battle. The emperor made Tokugawa the *shogun*, or military governor. His descendants had held that title ever since, ruling from their castle in the city of Edo.

The emperor lived in the city of Kyoto, where he attended to more important matters. Each year he would ask his ancestor, the sun goddess Amaterasu, to continue to protect the land she had founded.

Between the emperor's city and the shogun's city stretched what was then the world's busiest highway—the Tokaido Road. Thousands of travelers set their feet on the sand-and-stone road each day. Merchants and artisans carried silk, tea, pottery, and shiny lacquered boxes in backpacks or on mules. Pilgrims made the journey to one of Japan's sacred shrines, hoping the *kami* who lived there would bestow a blessing or a favor. Occasionally, samurai rode by on their horses. The shogun forbade all carts and carriages on the road, so that their wheels would not create ruts in the smooth gravel.

On this particular day, a girl and her father stopped to rest by the side of the road. Along came a *kago,* a passenger-box carried on poles by two husky men wearing loincloths. Inside the kago was a boy about to become a man, about to step inside his dreams. . . .

On the Tokaido Road

Seikei was tired of riding. The kago swayed back and forth endlessly, making him feel dizzy and sick. Though the floor was lined with silk pillows, the summer heat made the air inside the kago hot and sticky. Seikei slid open the bamboo door and peered outside.

A girl and an older man were sitting under a pine tree by the side of the road. The girl had removed her sandals and was rubbing her feet. Just at that moment, she looked up and met Seikei's eyes. Embarrassed, he quickly drew his head inside the kago.

Seikei wished the girl hadn't seen him. He felt ashamed to be carried along like some precious cargo. He would have gladly walked. He wanted to see the countryside and enjoy the views of the sea and mountains. But his father would not permit that.

Seikei's father was a tea merchant from Osaka, the third of Japan's major cities. He was going to Edo to open a new branch of his prosperous firm, and he took Seikei, his eldest son, along to learn the business. It was important to make a good impression, Seikei's father said. They should not enter Edo on foot, like laborers in search of work.

Remembering this, Seikei sighed and picked up the abacus that Father had given him. The abacus was a wooden frame with rods that held strings of beads. Those who were skilled in its use could rapidly calculate the prices, profits, and inventory needed to run a business.

Seikei despised the abacus. He would much rather have written poetry. At school, he had won a prize for writing a *haiku*. But his father had not been pleased. "Writing haiku is a talent expected of a samurai," Father had said.

Seikei understood. He could never be a samurai. The only way was to be a member of a samurai family.

Even though Seikei's father was wealthy, owned a fine house, and traveled in a kago, he would never be the equal of a samurai. Nor would his children or their children. They would remain merchants, rich or poor, all their lives. And so it was far more important for Seikei to learn to use an abacus than to write haiku.

Seikei's thoughts went back again to the girl he had seen. In spite of his efforts to concentrate on the abacus, the words of a haiku began to form inside his head:

A girl's feet are sore.
A merchant in a kago.
How lazy he is!

Hours later, Seikei was relieved when he felt the kago-bearers stop. As they set their burden on the ground, he opened the door and stepped out. It was good to stretch his legs, but he saw immediately that the journey was not yet over.

They had reached a checkpoint in the road. The shogun's officials were stopping everyone to ask what reason they had for traveling. And the wait would be a long one, for the road was choked with people waiting to be questioned by the officials.

Dozens of pilgrims were making the journey to Ise, Japan's holiest shrine. They were led by Buddhist priests and nuns, who tolled prayers on the strings of beads they wore over their orange robes. Two beggars moved through the crowd, holding their bowls out for offerings.

The large kago that held Seikei's father immediately attracted their attention. Seikei saw the door slide open, and his father's hand drop coins into the bowls. Father believed in giving to the needy. He regularly made sacrifices at Buddhist temples, as well as at the shrines of the older Shinto religion. Most Japanese did the same. As Seikei's father had told him, "All religions may have some truth to them. We must be sure not to offend any of the gods. Particularly since we have been favored with wealth."

Seikei looked at the sky. Storm clouds had blown in from the sea, and it would soon rain. He hoped they could pass through the checkpoint before the storm, for it would turn the road muddy and make the journey longer.

Behind him, Seikei heard the sound of approaching hoofbeats. As he turned, he saw horsemen holding bright banners with the *mon*, or crest, of a samurai family. "Make way!" they shouted. Seikei dropped to his knees and bowed his head. The pilgrims at the checkpoint moved quickly to the side of the road and did the same. It was unwise to fail to show a samurai proper respect.

Cautiously, Seikei raised his eyes as the hoofbeats passed. There were about twenty horsemen. All of them wore the two swords that marked them as samurai. But it was clear that one of them was a *daimyo*, or lord, who commanded the others. He wore red leather armor and a *hachimaki*, or headband, that was decorated with his family crest: a fish inside a red square. For some reason, Seikei's eyes went to the powerful right hand that the man used to hold the reins of his horse. On two of the fingers were massive golden rings.

Seikei only caught a glimpse of the man's face, but it was enough to see harsh eyes and a mouth that was scowling cruelly at the delay. Seikei shivered.

Then, out of the corner of his eye, Seikei saw one of the beggars straighten up and hold out his bowl. "A great man is generous!" the beggar cried.

Seikei watched, too fascinated to avert his gaze. He saw the samurai flick his reins slightly. Without a break in step, his horse instantly swerved toward the beggar. The man would be crushed beneath its hooves.

Then something extremely strange happened. Seikei could not believe his eyes. The beggar did a back-flip as easily as acrobats Seikei had seen in Osaka. The samurai's horse trampled across the spot where the beggar had knelt only a second before.

The samurai went on, seeming not to notice. But two of his men, following him, touched the hilts of their swords. Seikei held his breath. He knew that if a samurai drew his sword, he was obliged by honor to use it. Their razor-sharp swords, made by the most honored craftsmen in Japan, could cut a man's head off as easily as if it were a melon. Seikei had heard of that happening even in Osaka.

However, seeing that their master had passed by and that the beggar posed no threat to him, the samurai did not draw their swords. They kicked the sides of their horses and rode on. The beggar, crouched on his haunches, gave them a terrible look. Seikei saw his face turn into a mask of hatred, and noticed that the man had a long scar on the right side of his face. He was glad that the samurai did not see that look. The beggar must be a madman!

Seikei crept into his father's kago and told what he had seen. Father shook his head. "All sorts of people are found on the road," he said. "Robbers, swindlers, even Kirishitans."

Kirishitans? Over a century before, the shogun had banned the foreign religion, and executed all the Japanese who followed it. Seikei had never seen a Kirishitan, but rumors said that some of them still secretly practiced their mysterious faith.

"You see," Father went on, "how fortunate we are to be able to travel comfortably and safely in a kago."

"Still," said Seikei, "it would be much better to be a samurai. To have everyone make way for you, bow as you pass by . . . and to carry the two swords for battle."

"For battle?" Seikei's father snorted. "There have been no battles since the time of Ieyasu, the first Tokugawa shogun. The samurai only use swords on impudent people who do not know their place in life." He shook his finger at Seikei. "Like merchants' sons who occupy their minds with poetry."

Seikei bowed his head. His father knew him well. And probably he was right. But still . . . Seikei dreamed.

-2-

The Inn

Seikei and his father finally passed through the checkpoint. A short time later, they entered the town of Kameyama, where they planned to spend the night. There were many inns here, and in front of each one stood beautiful girls who called to the travelers who passed by. Each girl urged them to stay at the inn she worked for. "Best food in Kameyama!" some called. "Many servants to see to all your needs," said others. Two of the girls saw Seikei looking out from his kago. They smiled prettily and gestured for him to stop. When he slid the door shut quickly, he heard them giggling.

Seikei knew that Father would not stop for these girls. He had made plans for the trip long before they set out. He had a map that unfolded to show each section of the road, and had marked on it the towns and inns where he planned to stay. Father had asked other merchants who had made the trip where the most comfortable places were.

But when the bearers put Seikei's kago down, he saw that three samurai guarded the front gate of this inn. They wore the crest of the powerful daimyo they had seen at the checkpoint.

Seikei's father stepped out of his kago and bowed deeply. The samurai took no notice. The gate of the inn opened and a man wearing a plain blue kimono came out. "Konnichi-wa!" he said, greeting Seikei's father with a bow. He was the innkeeper.

"Konoike Toda," said Seikei's father, giving his family name first, as Japanese did. "A tea merchant from Osaka. Merchants there speak well of your inn."

"I am honored," the innkeeper said. "You see there are guards here. We have an important guest, a daimyo, Lord Hakuseki. I am afraid I cannot offer you our best rooms." He shrugged. "I can recommend another inn, if you wish."

Seikei's father leaned close to the man and whispered something that Seikei could not hear. The innkeeper smiled and bowed. He made a quick gesture with his hand, and two women immediately appeared in the doorway. They took the traveling cases from the kagos. Seikei and his father followed them into the inn, slipping off their sandals at the door.

Their room was in fact quite large and clean. The floor was large enough for at least four *tatami* sleeping mats, though they needed only two. "What did you say to the innkeeper?" Seikei asked.

"I promised him large thank-money," his father replied. "Comfort can usually be arranged, if one follows the polite way."

Seikei understood. To father, being polite meant offering enough money to get what he wanted. Not like a samurai, who would have slept in the open air rather than offer money to the greedy innkeeper.

Seikei and his father went to the bathhouse that was attached to the inn and soaked themselves in wooden tubs. The warm water soothed Seikei's bottom, still sore from being bounced around in the kago all day.

After they returned to their room, the two serving women brought trays with fish, rice, and tea. The food—especially the tea—was not of the best quality. Father sighed audibly a few times, but made no comment. Seikei ate his meal silently. He wanted to go out afterward and see the town, but knew that Father would probably disapprove of the idea.

Father loosened the *obi* around his waist as he finished his meal. He yawned, and Seikei knew it was useless to suggest leaving the inn. A voice sounded outside the sliding screen that served as a door to the room. Father called out permission to enter.

The innkeeper stood there, bowing. "I hope the meal was satisfactory," he said.

"It was adequate," Father replied. Seikei hid a smile.

He knew father feared that the innkeeper wanted more thank-money. "Now we are tired, and were just about to go to bed."

"Did I understand you to say you are a tea merchant?" the innkeeper said.

Father nodded.

"My honored guest, Lord Hakuseki, has expressed his desire for some fine tea," the innkeeper said. "The inn's tea is not of the quality he is used to."

To Seikei's surprise, Father replied, "I am sure he would find my tea quite ordinary. It is not meant for a daimyo."

The innkeeper paused for a moment. "I would not like to tell him you refused. It might seem rude."

Father spread his hands. "In that case, I will of course let him examine what I have. My son must bring it from my kago. Please leave us so that I can instruct him."

After the innkeeper departed, Seikei said, "Father, this is a wonderful opportunity!"

Father smiled ruefully. "When you have more experience, you will know better," he said. "Daimyos make very poor customers. They expect to buy everything at the lowest prices—that is, unless they force you into making a gift of your wares."

Father began to instruct Seikei carefully as to which tea he should bring. "Bring a box of the black tea from Nagano, and another box of the smaller black leaves from Tauyama. Lastly, a small portion of green tea that the farmer near Himeji ships us."

"You have better tea than that, Father," Seikei said. "What about—"

"I don't need you to tell me about tea," Father snapped. "The daimyo won't know the difference. Now go!"

Seikei went around to the back of the inn where the kagos had been left. The bearers were supposed to be guarding them, but were nowhere to be seen. Hearing the sounds of music and voices from a nearby tavern, Seikei guessed where they had gone.

When he returned with the tea, he found that Father had changed into a better kimono. After making sure Seikei had brought the correct tea, Father said, "Would you like to come along?"

Seikei nodded eagerly. He had not dared to ask.

"It will do you good to see what a daimyo is really like," Father said. "Chase some of those ideas about samurai out of your head."

Seikei quickly slipped off his travel-kimono and put on the one his mother had told him to wear when meeting customers.

The innkeeper nodded approvingly when he saw them. He led them to Lord Hakuseki's quarters, and motioned for them to kneel as he knocked on the door. When the door opened, they bowed their heads and moved across the floor on their knees.

13

"Well? Is this the tea merchant?" came a loud voice. "You may face me."

Seikei raised his eyes. Lord Hakuseki sat cross-legged on a platform in the center of the room. His two swords rested by his side. He was the same daimyo who had ridden by them at the checkpoint that afternoon. Seikei even recognized the two golden rings that the daimyo had worn. Now he was dressed in a magnificent red silk kimono with the fish crest embroidered on it. Standing around the walls of the room were four young samurai, and at the daimyo's feet were three servant women.

Lord Hakuseki prodded one of them with his foot. "Bring me their tea." As the woman took the three boxes, Father began to explain the different qualities of each one.

The daimyo pointed a finger at him. "If that man speaks again, cut his tongue out," he said to one of the guards. Father lowered his head humbly and bent forward on his hands and knees.

Lord Hakuseki looked inside each box, smelling the contents. Then he licked his finger and poked it inside one of them. Drawing it out, he tasted the tea leaves that clung to it. Seikei was glad that Father could not see how crudely the daimyo was testing his wares.

But the daimyo seemed pleased. He handed the box to the servant. "Make some tea with this," he told her.

As she left the room, Lord Hakuseki noticed Seikei watching him. Instantly, Seikei lowered his eyes, but the daimyo said, "You, boy! Come here!"

Seikei obeyed, moving forward on his knees. The daimyo reached down and pulled his head up by the hair. "How much do you think I should pay your master for the tea?"

Seikei struggled to think of a proper answer. When he spoke, his voice squeaked. "Whatever you think is fair, Lord."

Lord Hakuseki grunted and released his grip. "Stay here, then," he said. "I'll see how it tastes."

He looked at the innkeeper. "Take the merchant away. I don't want to see him again. I thought you were going to bring me some paper."

"At once, Lord," the innkeeper said. He and Father backed out of the room. Father glanced at Seikei for a second, but Seikei did not need the warning in his eyes. He moved back against one of the walls, hoping the daimyo wouldn't question him further.

In a few seconds, the door opened again. The innkeeper entered, followed by a girl carrying a box. Seikei blinked. He recognized the girl. She was the one who met his eyes when he opened the kago door on the road.

She was beautiful, he thought. As she knelt and bowed to the daimyo, Seikei could see her neck, long and graceful. Her black hair was held in place with a simple polished brown stick.

The daimyo commanded her to rise. Her face was heart-shaped and her eyes shone like pebbles at the bottom of a stream. She must be as afraid as I was, thought Seikei, but she shows no sign of it.

Lord Hakuseki seemed amused. "*You* are the paper-maker?" he asked her.

"My family has made paper for many generations," she explained. "I am traveling to Edo with my father to sell our wares, but he is ill and in need of rest."

Lord Hakuseki frowned. "I need paper fine enough to write a message for the shogun," he said. "You understand? The shogun himself. I am bringing him a gift, and I wish to enclose a suitable poem with it."

The girl nodded, saying nothing. She took several sheets of paper from her box and placed them on the platform in front of the daimyo. From where he sat, Seikei could see that each sheet was different. Most were white, though their textures ranged from very smooth to some that were as rough as pine bark. A few sheets were delicately colored, and the daimyo picked one of them up.

It was pink, rosy as the first light in the sky at dawn. "Unusual," Lord Hakuseki said, rubbing the paper between his fingers. Seikei saw the girl clench her fists, and then put them behind her back. She must feel the same way as he had when the daimyo tasted the tea.

"Ink," called out Lord Hakuseki. One of the servants knelt down and rubbed an ink-stick against a

16

stone tray. She poured a little water into the tray, mixing it with the dry ink.

A second servant brought a writing-brush to the daimyo, who took the cap off and swished the brush in the ink. Without pausing to test the darkness of the ink on a cloth, he dabbed it roughly onto the pink paper. He wrote too slowly, Seikei saw. Masters of the art always made swift, confident brushstrokes.

The girl was watching him too. Seikei saw her purse her lips in silent disapproval.

The daimyo stopped, and admired his work. He showed it to the girl. "Have you ever seen a poem written by a master?" he asked her.

Seikei saw her hesitate. Finally she nodded. "Basho used paper made by my great-grandparents to write his poetry. We have one of his poems at home. It was a gift from him."

Basho! Japan's greatest poet! Seikei felt envious.

Lord Hakuseki merely grunted. "And how would you say mine compares to his?"

The girl's mouth tightened into a line. That was the only sign that she was trying to control herself. "It is different, Lord. Yours displays your character, as the brush-writing of a master should."

Seikei put his hand to his mouth to hide a smile. A Japanese saying was: "A man and his brush-writing are one and the same." Even from where he sat, Seikei could see that the daimyo's writing was clumsy and crude.

But the daimyo seemed pleased by the girl's answer. "Would you like me to read it to you?" he asked.

The girl's eyes flashed at him in surprise for a second. Then she lowered them and nodded.

"The cherry blossoms cover the ground," he read, "like the heads of my enemies."

She murmured softly, as if admiring it.

"It just popped into my head," Lord Hakuseki said. "I think I was inspired by you."

The girl sat motionless on her heels.

"Because you are like a little cherry blossom yourself," the daimyo added. He looked around the room, and his samurai laughed.

The girl still did not move. Seikei felt sorry for her, but he admired her self-control.

The daimyo leaned forward. "Would you like to see something even more beautiful?" he asked the girl.

She nodded. Seikei could sense her embarrassment, but obviously the daimyo could not.

The daimyo gestured to one of his samurai, who brought him a small hinged box. Seikei marveled at its beauty. Covered with shiny black lacquer, it was decorated with tiny golden leaves.

Lord Hakuseki opened the box and held it out for the girl to see. Inside, on a bed of black silk, was a brilliant red stone, as dark as blood. The girl's eyebrows rose.

"What do you think of that?" the daimyo asked.

She shook her head. "I have never seen anything like it."

"Of course you haven't," said the daimyo. "It comes from a place far away, farther than China. It's called a ruby. I am bringing it to Edo as my gift to the shogun."

The girl said nothing, and Lord Hakuseki abruptly snapped shut the lid of the box. "Now the paper," he said. "How many sheets do you have?"

She blinked. "Of this paper?"

"The pink writing paper," the daimyo said impatiently. "I like it. How many sheets do you have?"

"My mother colors it with berries that she gathers in the mountains in the fall," she said. "They are hard to find."

Lord Hakuseki waved his hand. "I don't care about that. How many sheets?"

"We have twenty sheets," she said.

The daimyo opened a pouch that hung at his belt. He took two coins from it and handed them to the girl. Seikei saw a flash of gold as she closed her hand. "You are very generous, Lord," she said.

The daimyo pointed to one of his samurai. "Go with her and bring the paper," he said. The girl backed out of the room, looking relieved.

As she left, the servant woman returned with a pot of tea. Seikei tensed, remembering what he was waiting for. He watched as the woman poured the daimyo a cup.

The daimyo didn't pick it up. He was still examining the pink writing paper with his poem on it. Then he looked down, as if noticing the steaming tea for the first time. He raised it to his lips, and Seikei held his breath.

Lord Hakuseki put the cup down and returned his attention to the paper. Seikei looked around and caught the eye of one of the samurai guards. The man shook his head slightly. Seikei waited.

At last Lord Hakuseki looked around the room, and saw Seikei kneeling by the wall. "What are you here for?" he asked.

Seikei bowed his head, trying to act the way the girl had. "The tea, Lord," he mumbled.

"Oh, yes." Lord Hakuseki beckoned to one of his guards. "Give him some coins," he said.

The samurai took a few silver pieces from his kimono and handed them to Seikei. Dismayed, Seikei bowed humbly and made his way out of the room.

-3-

A Ghost Story

Father was not as disappointed as Seikei thought he would be. "What can you expect?" he said, shrugging. "This is not so bad. At least he paid you, and we didn't give him our best tea. Now, let's go to bed."

"Father, I cannot sleep," said Seikei. "I am too excited."

"We have another long day of travel tomorrow," Father said.

"I can sleep in the kago."

"Well, I cannot," Father said. "I must get my rest."

"There is a terrace at the back of the inn," said Seikei. "Could I go there to look at the view until I feel tired?"

Father shrugged. "If you wish," he said. "But do not leave the inn. The streets of this town are dangerous at night."

Seikei left, promising that he would not stay long.

When he reached the terrace, he found that rain had started to fall softly. Though the stone floor was covered with mats, it felt cool through his cotton *tabi*, or socks.

He walked to the railing that overlooked a small pond. The rain clouds had covered the moon and only a soft glow fell onto the water. He didn't mind the rain falling on his head. He felt feverish from his experience in the daimyo's quarters. I was afraid, he admitted to himself, just to be in his presence.

He jumped at the sound of a footstep just behind him. He whirled and saw the girl.

"I'm sorry," she said. "Did I startle you?"

"No," he said hastily. "I mean, I didn't expect to find someone here."

"Should I leave?" she asked.

It was hard for Seikei to speak. The girl seemed even more beautiful than she had before. "No, please," he said. "Stay."

"Was your master pleased with the paper?" she asked.

Seikei was confused. "Who?"

"The daimyo. I saw you in his room."

Now he understood. "No, no. I was there for the same reason you were. My father is a tea merchant. Excuse me. My name is Konoike Seikei."

She bowed. "I am called Michiko. My family name is Ogawa."

"Is it true that your family knew the poet Basho?"

She smiled, and he realized that it was rude to question her honesty.

"I ask," he said, "only because I greatly admire Basho's poetry."

Michiko put her hand over her mouth to hide her smile. Seikei knew why she was amused. Because he was a merchant's son, and merchants care for nothing except money.

He looked away from her, feeling ashamed. Then his eyes fell upon the pond, and he remembered one of Basho's poems. Seikei took a deep breath, and began to recite:

Clouds come from time to time—
and bring to men a chance to rest
from looking at the moon.

The girl clapped her hands. "That was the same poem I was thinking of before you appeared."

Seikei turned back to see her smile. He realized that she was not mocking him. Without thinking, he blurted out his secret wish: "I would so much like to be a samurai like Basho, and devote my life to poetry."

Michiko nodded. "But you do not have to be a samurai for that," she said. "Anyone can write poetry, if they wish."

"My father says it is not something a merchant should do. Only a samurai, and I can never be a samurai."

"I do not believe that," Michiko said. "Did you hear the poem that the daimyo wrote?"

"Yes."

"And did you see his brush-writing?"

Seikei nodded.

"So you know," Michiko said, "that although he is a samurai he does not have a noble spirit."

Seikei was surprised by the girl's boldness. "He was rude to you," he said. "I admired your courage."

"You thought I was courageous?" She shrugged. "I only reminded myself that my family needed to sell the paper."

Seikei nodded.

"It is true that Basho was a samurai," Michiko said. "But he discarded his swords. Isn't it Basho's spirit that we admire in his poetry? Though you are a merchant's son, you can still develop a noble spirit—brave, honest, and faithful to your family. And if you do, who can stop you from writing poetry?"

Seikei had no answer. He wondered how his father would reply.

They stared across the pond for a while. The sound of laughter came across the water from the other side.

"Some traveling *kabuki* are giving a play at the monastery," Michiko said. "I wanted to see it, but my father has been feeling ill all day. I used some of the gold the daimyo gave me to buy herbal tea for his stomach."

"I have never seen a kabuki play," Seikei said. "Father says they are improper."

"I think they are exciting," Michiko said. "Some are very scary, with goblins and ghosts."

"I like ghost stories," said Seikei.

"Do you? I know one that Basho told to my grandmother when she was a child. Would you like to hear it?"

"Very much," he replied.

"I will see if I can frighten you," she teased. "Let us go under the roof, so that the rain won't fall on us."

Seikei had forgotten about the rain. He would gladly have stood there all night to listen to this girl.

They sat down where the overhanging roof gave shelter. It was darker here, and the girl's face disappeared in the shadows. Seikei could hear only her voice.

"Well, then," she began. "Long ago, a Buddhist priest named Kokushi was traveling alone through the mountains. It was getting dark, and he had lost his way. He came upon a little hut, like the ones hermits sometimes live in to meditate on the Buddhist teachings.

"An old man opened the door when Kokushi knocked. He wore the orange robe of a Buddhist monk, but it was faded and worn. The monk refused to let Kokushi stay with him, but said there was a village on the other side of the hill. There, Kokushi could find food and lodging.

"Kokushi found this to be true. But in the village, no one answered his knock. All the houses seemed to be empty. Finally, he found the people gathered in one house, weeping and praying.

"The head of the village had died that day. His body lay in this house, and everyone had brought offerings of food to see him into the next life.

"The village had no priest, and Kokushi offered to perform the Buddhist rites for the man's soul. But the dead man's son said that no one could remain in the village on the night after a death. 'Strange things happen on that night,' he said, 'and it would be better if you came with us to the next village.'

"Kokushi replied that he had no fear. He would be glad to keep watch over the old man's body. The others tried to persuade him to leave, but he would not.

"At last, they departed, leaving him alone with the body. Kokushi said the Buddhist prayers and blew out all the lamps except one next to the body. He sat quietly meditating, but he was curious about what strange things might happen.

"Hours passed, and Kokushi began to doze. Suddenly, he realized that something else had entered the house. A mist gathered around the dead body. Kokushi saw the face of a horrible demon emerge from the mist. It was a horned beast, with ferocious teeth flashing in the mist. The demon lifted the body with its claws and began to devour it.

"As quickly as a cat swallows a mouse, the demon

26

ate everything—hair, bones, even the shroud. And this monstrous creature, after consuming the body, turned to the food offerings and ate them also. Then it went away as silently as it had come.

"In the morning, the villagers returned. They did not seem surprised to find that the body had disappeared. The dead man's son told Kokushi, 'Now you know why it is a law in our village that everyone must leave on the night after a death. But you are unharmed, and so must be a holy man.'

"Kokushi asked, 'Why do you not have the monk on the hill perform the funeral service for your dead?'

"The villagers did not understand him. 'There is no monk living near our village.' they said. 'For many years now, we have had no priest, for all fled when they saw what you have seen.'

"Kokushi took his leave, and walked back the way he had come. He found the little hut, and again knocked on the door. When it opened, the monk covered his eyes and said, 'Ah! I am so ashamed.'

" 'You need not be ashamed for refusing me shelter,' Kokushi said. 'I was very kindly treated in the village.'

"The monk replied, 'I am ashamed because you saw me in my true form. It was I who devoured the corpse and the offerings last night before your eyes. For I am a *jikininki*—an eater of human flesh.'

"The monk explained that he once had been a priest, the only one for miles around. 'The people would bring me their dead so that I might pray over them. But I greedily ate the offerings that they had brought for the dead to enjoy. And when I died, as punishment I was sent back to earth as a jikininki.' He hung his head. 'Now all men must flee from the sight of me, or they will die.'

" 'Yet I saw you,' said Kokushi, 'and I did not die.'

" 'You must be a holy man,' the jikininki said. 'I beg you, pray for me so that I may be released from this hideous state of existence.'

"Kokushi began to say the proper Buddhist prayers, and when he looked up, the monk had vanished, along with the little hut in which he lived. Kokushi found himself alone in the grass, next to a tombstone covered with moss. It was a *go-rin-ishi,* the stone that marks the grave of a priest."

"Did you ever hear this story before?" Michiko asked Seikei.

"No," Seikei said. "It was a good one, but I was not afraid."

"I must return to my father now," said Michiko. "Perhaps we will meet again, and then you can read me a poem you have written."

"I promise," said Seikei. He watched as she rose and went into the inn. How graceful she is, he thought.

After she left, a cool wind blew across the terrace, sending a chill through Seikei. The play across the lake was over, and now all was silent. He began to think of the jikininki, and stood up. It was too quiet and too dark. He had the odd feeling that something might be hiding in the darkness beyond the terrace. He didn't want to stay out here any longer.

-4-

The Hour of the Rat

Seikei hurried back to the room where his father was sleeping. He took off his kimono and lay down on the other mat.

But he didn't fall asleep. The inn was still noisy. Only rice-paper screens separated one room from another, and Seikei could hear Lord Hakuseki's men talking loudly in other rooms along the corridor. They were drinking rice wine, and showed no concern for the slumbers of the other guests.

Seikei heard his father snoring. All the noise did not disturb *his* sleep. Seikei knew that tomorrow would bring another long, uncomfortable trip in the kago. He sighed, and tried to shut the sounds out of his ears.

Then loud shouts made him sit up and listen. He could hear very clearly, though the voice was farther down the hallway. It was Lord Hakuseki himself. He was scolding one of the inn's servants for not bringing the wine quickly enough. The sound of a blow was followed by a muffled cry. Then heavy footsteps and a loud thud. The servant had been thrown out on the wooden floor of the hallway. Much laughter followed from the other samurai.

Truly, as the girl Michiko had said, this daimyo did not have a noble spirit. I would not be that way if I were a samurai, Seikei thought. He reminded himself of the three qualities of a samurai—loyalty, right conduct, and bravery. Right conduct meant setting an example for others to follow. Lord Hakuseki, powerful though he was, did not know the difference between right and wrong.

The noise of the partying continued for some time. Gradually, it began to die down. Seikei heard the slow footsteps of samurai going down the hall to the privy in the courtyard, and then returning. Finally, the inn became quiet.

Seikei tossed and turned, unable to get comfortable. He regretted telling the girl he liked ghost stories. Now he could not get the image of the jikininki out of his mind. The dim light from the corridor shone through the rice-paper walls of the room. The walls were decorated with a pattern of whorls and curlicues. Every time Seikei looked in their direction, he seemed to see large eyes staring at him.

Far off, a temple bell rang once, a hollow sound

that meant the first hour after midnight had begun—the Hour of the Rat. Seikei closed his eyes, but he could hear the sounds of heavy breathing all around him. He knew it was only the occupants of the rooms on either side. But it sounded like a gang of jikininkis waiting to gobble him up as soon as he fell asleep.

Then his body tensed. He heard another sound. Something was sliding across the floor outside the doorway. Seikei's eyes popped open, and he saw the bamboo-screen door begin to slide open, very, very slowly.

Seikei felt his hair stand on end. As he watched in horror, the door opened wide. Something was standing behind it—something larger than a man. The light in the hallway was too dim for Seikei to see anything more than a shadow. But he could see that it had a huge head, with horns sticking out of it.

Seikei sat up as quickly as if he had been a marionette on strings. He waved his arms wildly, and tried to say, "I'm not dead!" But his throat was paralyzed with fear, and only a squeak came out.

The shadow turned in his direction. Seikei saw its eyes flash in the light from the hallway. The creature's white face looked down on Seikei. It stared at him for a second and then raised one arm. Seikei saw a small object in its hand, red and glowing like a fiery eye. The ghostly form waved the red object toward him. To Seikei, it seemed like the spirit was trying to cast a spell on him.

The shadow moved backward, and the door slid closed again. Seikei felt as if he were made of stone. He could not move a muscle, but his heart was pounding so fast that he thought his chest would break open.

His ears were so keen now that he thought he could hear insects crawling in the corners of the room. As he listened, he heard a door sliding back. The ghost must be going into another room.

What should I do? Seikei asked himself. He must get up and raise an alarm. It would be his fault if the monster devoured some other sleeping person. Perhaps even the girl, Michiko. He clenched his fists, and thought of the first quality of a samurai—bravery. He must do it.

He forced himself to stand, but his legs were shaking and weak. Ignore weakness, he told himself. Move forward without thinking. He took a step toward the door.

When he reached it, he had to remind himself again not to think of danger. Death had no meaning to the samurai, he told himself, for that is the fate of all and it does not matter if it comes today or tomorrow.

He slid the door open, and looked out in the corridor. At the far end, where the darkness was deepest, he saw the shadow moving. Seikei again found that fear silenced his voice. He was angry at himself, and stamped his foot.

As soon as he did this, the shadow began to sink

into the floor. Seikei could hardly believe what he saw. Bit by bit, it shrank from sight until only its great horned head was visible. Then that disappeared as well. Nothing remained.

Seikei looked around. The corridor was empty and silent. All the doors were tightly closed. He walked to the place where the shadow had disappeared. There was a door beyond it, but he was sure it had not opened. Checking, he slid it aside and looked out. The rain had stopped, and the moon shone brightly over the courtyard beyond. Nothing was there.

Seikei went back to his own room and shut the door. He was calmer now, proud of himself for having been brave enough to follow the ghost. Perhaps when he stamped his foot, he had frightened it away.

He lay down on his mat again. The inn was peaceful. Once more he heard the sounds of snoring people. But they did not seem so fearful now. Something told him that the danger was gone. But what had it been? Why did it come to his door?

All night, he asked himself those questions. Finally, when the first twittering sparrows outside signaled the dawn, he fell asleep. But he did not rest for long.

~5~

Prisoners in the Inn

Early the next morning, angry shouts and the sounds of running footsteps woke everybody in the inn. Seikei kept his eyes firmly closed, hoping the noise would stop. Someone rapped on the bamboo frame at the doorway. Seikei heard his father get up to see what was happening.

It was the innkeeper. "I apologize for the disturbance," he said. "But my honored guest Lord Hakuseki has reported something missing from his room."

"We know nothing about it," said Seikei's father.

"I am sure," the innkeeper said. "But his men have surrounded the inn and will let no one leave."

"Are we prisoners, then?" asked Father angrily. "I am on an important journey. I must arrive in Edo in three days."

"I regret that the matter is beyond my control," the innkeeper replied. "We must wait for the judge to arrive."

"Bring us tea and something to eat at once," Father said. "Unless we are to be starved as well."

"I will see to it myself," said the innkeeper.

Father closed the door and rubbed his fingers through his hair, the way he did when he was angry. "Are you awake?" he asked Seikei. "Did you hear?"

"Yes, Father," Seikei mumbled. "Could I sleep a bit longer?"

"No. You will develop lazy habits, like the samurai you admire so much. See what trouble this one has caused us."

Seikei rose slowly. He wondered if he should tell his father what had happened during the night. It seemed like a dream now. No, he decided. Father was angry enough, and would only tell Seikei not to imagine foolish things.

A maid brought tea and a bowl of pickled vegetables. The sharp taste of the pickles helped to clear Seikei's head. Secretly, he was glad not to have to get inside the kago this morning. The innkeeper said that a judge was coming. Seikei thought it would be exciting to observe how he would investigate the crime.

There was a knock at the door. Seikei slid it open and saw another samurai, one who did not wear the crest of Lord Hakuseki's clan. "The judge commands you to come," he said. They followed him down the hallway to the large room that Lord Hakuseki had occupied the night before.

The judge now sat on the platform in the center of the room. He wore a brown kimono, embroidered with yellow chrysanthemums. The man was fat, but his eyes were as sharp as a cat's. He reminded Seikei of a statue of Buddha, except that the judge wore the swords of a samurai under his obi.

Lord Hakuseki and his men were seated along the walls of the room. The other guests of the inn filed in and sat on the floor in front of the magistrate. Michiko and her father sat right in front of Seikei. Seikei glanced at her shyly, and she smiled.

"I am Judge Ooka," the judge said in a voice that seemed surprisingly pleasant. "I am here to investigate the theft of a valuable object that belonged to Lord Hakuseki. Does anyone wish to confess to the crime?"

The room was silent. Seikei kept his eyes on the floor. He knew that anyone accused of a crime must admit his guilt before he could be punished. However, judges had the power to order a suspect to be tortured to force a confession. It would be far better for the guilty person to confess at once.

"Since no one has confessed," Judge Ooka said, "I will order my men to search your rooms to prove your innocence." Seikei heard his father sigh softly. He was probably worried that their belongings would be carelessly handled.

At the judge's nod, three of his assistants left the

room. "The object was taken while Lord Hakuseki was sleeping," he said. "Yet his guards outside saw no one enter or leave the inn. I ask anyone who heard anything strange during the night to speak."

Seikei lifted his head, but quickly lowered it again. However, Judge Ooka noticed, and looked in his direction. "Did you hear something?" he asked. Seikei did not know what to say.

It was his father who answered. "The inn was very noisy," he said. "Everyone must have heard sounds."

Another guest spoke up. "There was loud singing, and then an argument." A third guest added, "I heard someone being beaten." Seikei thought that many guests must have been annoyed by the noisy doings of Lord Hakuseki and his men. They were glad to be able to complain freely.

"You did not report this earlier," Judge Ooka said, looking at Lord Hakuseki. "Who was beaten?"

The daimyo shrugged. "A servant. He was careless, and I gave him a couple of knocks to teach him manners."

Judge Ooka asked the innkeeper, "Where is this servant?"

"I will bring him at once, Lord," the innkeeper said. He left the room and in a few seconds returned with a thin little man who lay face down on the floor in front of the judge. "Sit up so I can see your face," Judge Ooka said.

He looked at the servant's face. "I see you have a

bruise on your cheek," the judge said. "How did you get it?"

"It was my fault, Lord," the man said. "I was too slow and stupid, and I deserved a beating."

"You brought wine to Lord Hakuseki and his men, is that so?"

"Yes, that was my duty."

"When you came to this room, did you see this box?" Judge Ooka picked up the shiny black casket that had held the jewel.

"No, Lord, I saw nothing."

"Nothing? Nothing at all?"

The man hesitated. "I saw nothing I was not supposed to see."

"How long have you worked in this inn?"

"Two years."

"Then you must know it very well. You could probably find your way about the hallways in the dark, is that so?"

"Yes, Lord."

"You probably know many places in the inn where you could easily hide something small, is that so?"

The man did not reply. Judge Ooka went on, his voice as calm and gentle as if he were talking with a friend. "Suppose you found a gold coin in the street and wanted to hide it so no one could steal it from you. Where would you put it?"

"I would give the coin to a temple, Lord," the servant replied.

The judge nodded. "That would be virtuous." In the same tone, he added, "You know that I could have your arms tied behind your back and have them pulled upward until you confessed?"

The servant nodded. He was shaking now.

"Wouldn't it be better to confess at once and spare yourself that pain?" the judge said.

The servant lay on the floor again. "I have not stolen anything, Lord. I swear it."

Before the judge could reply, the door to the room slid open. One of his assistants entered, and Seikei saw that he carried the sample box of paper that Michiko had shown to Lord Hakuseki. The man strode forward and placed the box in front of Judge Ooka. "We have found the stolen jewel," he said. "It was hidden inside this box."

-6-

Looking for a Ghost

Lord Hakuseki pointed at Michiko and her father. "They are the thieves!" he shouted. "She tricked her way into my room and saw the jewel."

Judge Ooka gestured for them to come forward. Michiko put her hands to her face and knelt alongside her father. "This box belongs to you?" Judge Ooka asked.

"Yes," her father replied. "But we did not touch the jewel. I do not know how it got there."

"What is your name?" Judge Ooka asked.

"Ogawa Iori, a paper-maker from Kyoto."

"And this girl?"

"My daughter Michiko."

"She's a sly one," said Lord Hakuseki. "She asked me to show her the jewel."

Seikei stared at him. He was lying! He was violating the samurai code of honor.

"Let me see your face," Judge Ooka said to Michiko. His sharp eyes stared into hers. "You will receive only a light punishment if you tell the truth. Think carefully before you answer. Is this man really your father?"

"Oh yes, Lord."

"And did he tell you to ask to see the jewel?"

"No! No! We did not know there was any jewel here. I only showed our paper, and Lord Hakuseki wrote a poem and asked if I wanted to see something beautiful."

"Torture them," Lord Hakuseki said. "They'll soon tell the truth."

Judge Ooka ignored him. He took the ruby from the paper-box and held it out. "Is this the jewel that Lord Hakuseki showed you?"

Michiko nodded.

"Where did you go after you left his room?"

"I returned to our room."

"Did you stay there the rest of the night?"

"Yes," said Michiko's father. "We went right to sleep."

"No," said Michiko. "I could not sleep, and I went to the terrace to see the view." Her father groaned softly.

"But it was raining last night," said the judge.

"Yes. But it was quieter outside, and very pleasant."

"How long did you stay there?"

"Not very long."

Seikei waited for her to say that she had met him there, but after a moment, she added, "I soon went back to our room and fell asleep."

"Perhaps you stayed on the terrace until everyone else in the inn had gone to bed?"

"No, it was still noisy when I returned."

Judge Ooka frowned at her. "Can you explain how this jewel got into your room?"

"I do not know. But I did not take it."

The judge sighed. "Though you are only a child, this is a very serious crime. I must warn you that I can—"

"It wasn't her!" Seikei's voice rang out from behind Michiko. Everyone turned to look at him. Even his father was staring. But Seikei had to tell the truth. He could not let the girl be tortured.

"I saw the thief," Seikei went on. "It was a ghost, a jikininki. It had horns, and it opened the door of our room. It was holding the jewel in its hand."

Seikei's father jumped up. "Lord, you must excuse this boy, my son. He is fond of imagining things, and he has strange dreams." Father gave Seikei a ferocious look that told more than words could about the scolding he would get later.

"Come here," the judge commanded. Seikei went forward. His father followed, still explaining that Seikei could not be trusted to tell the truth, for he was only a half-witted child who read poetry.

"What did you call the thief?" said Judge Ooka. "A jikininki? Where did you hear of jikininkis?"

Seikei hesitated. "I was on the terrace when this girl came out. She told me a ghost story. But I really saw it. You must believe me. I was not dreaming."

"You see?" said Seikei's father. "He is very nervous. We had a long journey yesterday, and he is not used to travel. This girl may have enchanted him in some way. Who knows what kinds of people you will meet on the road? Thieves, beggars, madmen . . . I blame it on the innkeeper, for letting such people stay here."

"You were glad enough to find a room last night," the innkeeper shouted.

"The boy may have been one of the thieves," added Lord Hakuseki. "He saw the jewel too. They were all in it together."

Judge Ooka stood up. "I cannot think here," he said. "Hold all these people until I return," he told one of his assistants. Pointing to Seikei, he said, "You come with me." When Seikei's father began to protest, the judge silenced him with a wave of his hand.

Seikei was frightened. Perhaps the judge was taking him to be tortured. He regretted having spoken out, but he could not have remained silent.

"Show me where your room is," the judge said when they were in the corridor. Seikei led him there. "Where were you sleeping?" said the judge.

Seikei showed him. "Lie down, just as you were, and

tell me everything you saw," Judge Ooka said. He listened carefully as Seikei retold the story. "I heard the temple bell sound the Hour of the Rat," Seikei began. He went on to describe how the jikininki had waved the glowing red object at him.

"I shouted that I was alive," Seikei said.

"And then?" said the judge.

"The jikininki closed the door, because it knew I was alive and it could not eat me."

"Or because you were awake and saw it. What then?"

"I listened for a while, and didn't hear anything. But then I heard footsteps again."

"Jikininkis, being spirits, make no noise with their feet," the judge pointed out. "Nor would a careful thief, with so many guards around."

Seikei struggled to remember. "That's right. It wasn't footsteps. The sound I heard was another door sliding back. It made almost no noise, but I was listening hard."

"Another door." The judge nodded. "What did you do then?"

"I got up and looked out in the corridor."

The judge raised his eyebrows. "Weren't you frightened? You had just escaped being eaten."

Seikei nodded. "I was very frightened. But I . . ." Seikei thought the judge, who was a samurai himself, might be offended.

"Go on," said the judge.

"I reminded myself that a samurai is willing to face death without fear."

The judge put his hand over his mouth, but Seikei could see that his eyes were twinkling. Seikei felt his own face redden. Like his father, the judge thought he was foolish.

"Where did you learn that?" asked the judge.

"I read it in a book," Seikei said.

"A book by Daidoji Yuzan?" the judge asked.

"Yes." Seikei was surprised. "How did you know?"

"I read that book when I was a boy. Sometimes I still read it. We need not discuss that now. Stand here at the door, and tell me what you saw in the corridor."

Seikei went on with his story. "And when I stamped my foot, the jikininki sank into the floor and disappeared."

"Show me where."

Seikei went to the end of the corridor.

"Stamp your foot like you did last night," the judge said.

"I stamped in front of our door, not here," Seikei replied.

"I know. Stamp here now."

Seikei obeyed. "Now over here," said the judge. "Again, back there. Try this spot."

Judge Ooka heard something and squatted down on the floor. He began to run his hands along the smooth boards. He grunted, and stuck his finger into a knothole.

The board lifted up. Seikei stared. Underneath was a dark black hole that led down into the earth.

"Very good," said the judge. "Take off your kimono so that you will not get it dirty."

Seikei felt his body tingle. "You want me to go down there?"

"As you see, I am too fat to fit inside."

"But what if the thief is still there?"

This time, Judge Ooka did not hide his smile. "How could he do harm to you, if you do not fear death?"

-7-

In the Tunnel

Wearing only his cotton loincloth, Seikei wriggled into the hole, feet first. He slipped downward, and found that it was the entrance to a tunnel. He looked up and saw Judge Ooka's face. "It goes farther," Seikei said.

"Follow it to the end," the judge said, "and then be sure to come back and tell me where it comes out."

Seikei gritted his teeth. The judge did not seem to think there was any real danger. But Seikei was terrified. He moved forward only a step at a time, stretching his arms out to feel the walls of the tunnel. He had to stoop to keep his head from bumping overhead. He was in total darkness, and would be totally unprepared if something suddenly grabbed him with its claws or ripped into his body with sharp teeth.

In all the stories of samurai Seikei had read, he had

never heard of one burrowing under the earth. Some fought monsters under the sea or on lonely mountaintops. Others battled warriors in single combat and rode their horses against the armies of enemy daimyos. None of them crept through the damp ground like a worm. That was probably why the judge made *him* do it.

Seikei heard a sound, and realized that it was his own teeth chattering. It was cold here, and he began to think of graveyards and the spirits of the dead. Perhaps he really was pursuing a jikininki that rested by day in some hidden spot and rose at night to seek its victims.

And what would it do if Seikei disturbed its slumber?

He must not think of that. Death, he told himself again, has no meaning to a samurai. But it was more difficult to believe that now than it was during the night in the inn. There, at least, he could have cried out if the jikininki had attacked him. Many samurai guards had been sleeping nearby. Down here, if Seikei screamed, his voice would be swallowed up in the earth and never heard.

He stopped. He was breathing hard, although he had not moved fast. Go forward, he told himself. Do not give in to fear.

Little by little, he worked his way through the tunnel. He lost all track of time. Then he bumped up against a wall of earth. Once more, panic threatened to overcome him, and he fought it off. The tunnel must go somewhere.

Seikei felt around himself, and realized that there was room to stand upright. Over his head was another hole. He found handholds dug into the walls, and climbed to the top.

He felt a stone resting over the entrance. He pried his fingers around the edge and moved it to the side. He stuck his head out, breathing the fresh air. The sky had never looked so beautiful to him before.

As Seikei climbed out, he was astonished to see Judge Ooka walking toward him. With him was a man whose orange robe and shaved head identified him as a Buddhist monk.

"How did you know where the tunnel led?" Seikei asked.

"I was not sure of the exact location," the judge replied. "But your description of the thief gave me an idea. We are inside the temple grounds, where travelers who cannot afford lodging are permitted to rest. This monk has told me that last night, a group of actors put on a play here."

"Oh, yes. Michiko and I could hear them from the terrace of the inn. We wished we could see the play, and that was why she told me the story of the jikininki."

Judge Ooka put his hand on Seikei's shoulder. "I think you and I will attend more plays before we have solved the mystery of the ghost in the inn." He looked at Seikei's mud-smeared body. "You need a bath, but first let us return to finish this part of the business."

As they walked back, Seikei said, "The tunnel was very long. No one could have dug it in a single night."

The judge nodded. "You are observant. I think we will find that the theft of the jewel was not as simple as it first appeared."

They returned to the room where the others waited. Seikei's father seemed startled to see his son half-dressed and covered with mud. So did the innkeeper, who moved toward the doorway.

"Hold that man!" Judge Ooka called out to the guards. Two of them took hold of the innkeeper and forced him to his knees.

The judge settled himself on the platform. He picked up the jewel that had been found in the paper-seller's box, and showed it to Lord Hakuseki. "Are you certain that this is the object that was stolen from your room?"

"Of course. It is a gift for the shogun from my family."

Startling everyone, Judge Ooka smashed the jewel onto the wooden platform. It shattered into a thousand pieces. "False," he said. "A clever imitation made of glass, one that could be part of the costumes of a kabuki theater troupe."

Lord Hakuseki looked dazed as he stared at the fragments of red glass scattered on the floor. "But the jewel I had was genuine."

"Yes, and you would have taken this false one to the shogun. Imagine what his feelings would have been when he discovered that you had presented him with an imitation."

Lord Hakuseki looked around angrily. "Why did this paper-seller have it? Did he take the real jewel?"

"It was only by chance that it was placed in his room." The judge looked at Seikei's father. "It would have been discovered in *your* room, had your son not been awake when the thief opened the door. Instead he went to another room and placed it there, for it did not matter which room it was found in."

Judge Ooka looked at Lord Hakuseki. "That was the thief's plan. He knew that you would discover the theft and immediately raise a cry. The other rooms would be searched, and when the false jewel was discovered, you would be certain it was the real one. No one would look for the thief, since it would be thought he had already been found."

"How do you know all this?" asked Lord Hakuseki.

"This boy set me on the correct way of thinking," the judge replied. "After that, it was easy to see what really happened."

"But who is the thief? And where is my jewel?"

"Those things I have yet to discover," said the judge calmly. "I think this innkeeper may help me. Bring him forward."

The guards dragged the man before Judge Ooka. He looked sullenly at the floor.

"Why is there a tunnel between your inn and the monastery?" Judge Ooka asked him.

"I know nothing about it," the innkeeper said.

The judge turned to Lord Hakuseki. "Have you ever seen this man before? Think carefully."

The daimyo frowned. "I cannot remember. Of what importance is he to me?"

Judge Ooka looked at the daimyo. "You may have done him some injury."

"What of it? He is not a samurai. I have power over many people, all those who live on my lands. I can treat them as I wish. Show me that he has stolen my jewel, and I will order one of my men to kill him instantly."

"He is my prisoner, and you will not touch him," said the judge. "I speak with the authority of the shogun, for I am one of his officials." He nodded toward the guards. "Take this innkeeper away, and use methods to persuade him to speak." Seikei saw a look of fear appear on the man's face.

When they were gone, Judge Ooka sat thinking for a while. "The solution to this mystery will take time."

"I have no time," snapped Lord Hakuseki. "I am to appear before the shogun in four days."

"Then you should be on your way," said the judge. "I will arrive in the shogun's castle by that time to report what has happened." He turned to the other guests. "You are all free to go as well. But this boy must remain with me for the present."

Seikei's father spoke up. "He cannot have had anything to do with the theft, Lord. You said that yourself."

"He was a witness," said Judge Ooka. "And he is a bright, brave boy. I need his help."

Seikei's father put his hand to his head. "How can he possibly help you? I must warn you about him—"

"Put your mind at rest," said the judge. "You are on your way to Edo too? I will return him safely to you there."

Seikei's father shot a final look of warning at his son, and then left. Michiko came up to Seikei. "I owe you more than I can possibly repay," she said. "You saved my father and me from being tortured."

"I only told the truth," he said.

"Many people would have held their tongues," she told him. "You had no reason to risk your own safety."

"It is honorable to speak the truth without regard for the consequences," Seikei said.

Judge Ooka overheard him. "I see you remember that book well," he said. "Now come along. Have you ever ridden a horse?"

Seikei gasped. "Never, Lord."

"You must now. We are going to chase the thief."

-8-

A Sword for Seikei

Outside the inn, Judge Ooka and his men mounted their horses. The innkeeper, hands bound behind his back, was tied to a rope and forced to walk behind them. The judge turned and said to one of his guards, "Bunzo, teach this boy to ride a horse." Bunzo reached down and deftly swung Seikei onto the back of his saddle. Seikei threw his arms around the samurai and held on tightly. Even though they rode slowly, he bumped up and down hard. He thought that he would never be able to survive a long journey this way.

Fortunately, Judge Ooka's house was just outside the town, surrounded by a high stone wall. Inside the gate, they dismounted in a large courtyard. As the judge's men led the innkeeper away, Bunzo took Seikei to the stables.

Bunzo was a burly samurai with a mustache. Like all

samurai, he had shaved the hair above his forehead, and tied the top of his hair into a narrow roll. His clothes were spotless and neatly pressed. "Never rode a horse, eh?" Bunzo said.

Seikei shook his head.

Bunzo brought Seikei a plain brown coat, short pants that ended at the knee, black leggings that covered his legs and feet, and a pair of leather sandals. The leggings were tight and their thick rough cloth scratched Seikei's legs. As he walked gingerly about, Bunzo grinned. "Merchant's son, aren't you?"

"How can you tell?" said Seikei.

"You're used to soft clothes. That's what merchants wear. They get rich by selling at high prices, cheating people."

Seikei hung his head. That was why everybody looked down on merchants. They didn't grow food, like the farmers, or make things, like Michiko and her father did. They only sold goods.

Bunzo led a gray mare out of its stall. He showed Seikei how to saddle it. "This horse won't run," Bunzo said. "Too old. If you hit her to make her go fast, she'll just stop. All you have to do is stay on her."

He helped Seikei get into the saddle and showed him how to place his sandals in the stirrups. "If you want to turn right or left, just tug the reins a little bit," Bunzo said. "This horse has been riding a lot longer than you. She'll know where to take you."

Bunzo handed Seikei the reins. Nothing happened.

The horse turned its head and looked at Seikei. Even this horse knows I'm not a samurai, Seikei thought.

"Tell her to go," said Bunzo. "Move forward in the saddle."

"Go, go," shouted Seikei. The horse began to walk back toward the stable.

"Turn her now," said Bunzo. "Use the reins like I told you."

Seikei yanked the reins—too hard, for the horse jerked her head and shook her back so roughly that Seikei lost his balance. He let go of the reins and grabbed the horse's neck to keep from falling off.

Bunzo took hold of Seikei's coat and pulled him upright. "Sit with your back straight," he said. "Think of yourself as part of the horse. When she moves, you move with her."

Seikei began to get the idea. After some more practice, he was able to turn the horse. It was exciting to sit up here, high above the ground. He closed his eyes for a second, imagining himself in the armor of a samurai. Then the horse turned suddenly when he did not expect it, and Seikei fell off.

Bunzo walked over and picked Seikei out of the dust. He plopped him back into the saddle.

"You know, Judge Ooka is a very wise man," Bunzo said. "No criminal ever escapes him. He sees things that others do not notice. But once in a while, even he makes a mistake."

Seikei blushed. He knew who the mistake was. He

gritted his teeth and resolved that he would never lose his balance again.

Judge Ooka appeared in the courtyard. "How is the training coming along?" he said. "You know, Bunzo, this young man wishes he could be a samurai."

Bunzo rolled his eyes and said nothing.

"He needs a sword, don't you think?" the judge said.

Seikei held his breath. Only in his dreams had he dared imagine anything like this.

"He is not a samurai," Bunzo said disapprovingly.

"Perhaps a wooden sword," said the judge.

Bunzo shrugged. "At least he would not cut himself."

"Let us go find one," said the judge. He turned to Seikei and said, "Perhaps you would enjoy a bath right now."

Seikei realized that he was still muddy from his trip through the tunnel, and that after the lessons he also smelled of horse.

The judge pointed. "Go around to the back of the house and you will find the bath. I will join you there."

Seikei left the judge talking with Bunzo. He found the bath, removing his sandals before entering. An older woman met him inside the doorway. "Judge Ooka told me to wash myself," Seikei told her shyly.

She motioned toward a large shallow pool lined with green tiles. It was empty, but the woman pointed to a bamboo tube plugged with a cork. "Open that, and water will come," she said. She closed the door, and Seikei undressed and sat down in the bath. He pulled out the cork, and water began to flow. To his surprise, it was warm. In his home in Osaka, his family heated water on the cooking stove when they wished to take warm baths. He sat back and enjoyed feeling the water flow over his body.

Soon afterward, the judge arrived. He joined Seikei in the bath, which was large enough to hold at least ten people without crowding. Unless all of them were as large as Judge Ooka. As he settled into the bath, the level of the water rose enough to flow over the sides.

"Why is a hot bath such a pleasure?" the judge asked.

Seikei had never thought about it. "It just feels good," he said.

"Perhaps that is the best answer," said the judge. "To enjoy, and not question it. But as I grow older, my mind becomes more restless. I seek out answers to things."

"Why is the water so warm?" asked Seikei, thinking that the judge would be pleased with another question.

He was, nodding approvingly. "There is a hot spring nearby," he explained. "When I heard of it, I realized that its water could be channeled here through bamboo tubes. Much easier than heating water on a stove and carrying it in buckets."

The judge closed his eyes and sunk deeper into the

water. "I regret that we cannot stay here for long. We must soon pursue the thief."

Seikei had been wondering about that. It seemed to him that while they delayed, the thief must be getting farther away. But Judge Ooka must know something about the thief by now.

"Did the innkeeper confess?" asked Seikei.

"He would not talk," said the judge, "although some of my men showed him the instruments of torture. So we left him alone with a sword, and he committed *seppuku.*"

"What? He killed himself? But that means you can't learn anything from him."

"Oh, no. He told me all I really need to know. Except for a few details, which we will surely discover in time."

Seikei blinked. The judge must be testing his loyalty. Surely he could not have solved the crime already.

The judge saw the look on Seikei's face, and smiled. "Why would a man kill himself rather than confess to a crime?" the judge asked him. "The penalty for theft is not death."

Seikei thought about it. "To protect someone else?" he suggested.

"Very good. And what sort of man would choose death rather than betray his friends?"

"A samurai?"

The judge nodded. "If he were of noble spirit. But why would a samurai be working as an innkeeper?"

Seikei could not answer that. Judge Ooka rose from the bath and began to dry himself. "Come. You can think about these questions later. Now you must receive your sword."

Seikei dressed hastily. Even if it were only a wooden sword, he thought, it was more than he could have dreamed of.

The judge led him into the garden at the back of the house. Like everything else in the judge's home, the garden indicated a love of beauty. Plants and trees surrounded a large rectangle of neatly raked white gravel. A few stones of different shapes and sizes were resting here and there on the gravel.

Seikei had seen gardens like this in Zen Buddhist temples in Kyoto. The monks gazed at them for hours, to clear their minds.

The judge sat on a wooden bench at the edge of the garden, motioning Seikei to sit beside him. Seikei knew that the stones were placed to fool the eye. Gazing at them long enough, you began to feel you were looking out on a vast landscape.

Indeed, it seemed that way. He could easily imagine the distant rocks as mountains and think of himself walking the raked lines in the sand, so tiny that he could not be seen. It would be a long journey.

Suddenly, the judge clapped his hands loudly, twice. He was summoning the *kami,* the spirits of nature that live all over Japan. The judge looked at Seikei, and he realized that he was expected to clap too.

Something strange happened when Seikei clapped his hands. The garden changed slightly, in ways almost too subtle to notice. A little breeze stirred up some of the grains of sand. The rocks in the distance seemed to move farther away. The back of Seikei's neck tingled.

"We are going on a journey," the judge said. "We ask you to guide our steps and help us accomplish our purpose. This boy needs to learn many things. I will teach him what I can, but when I fail you must show him the way. Look upon him with kindness."

The little breeze died down, and the garden was calm and silent once more. The judge rose to his feet, and as Seikei turned, he saw a wooden sword resting on a stand behind them.

Bunzo must have placed it there, but Seikei had heard no sound. The judge picked up the sword. Seikei saw that the smooth, dark wood was polished to a high gloss. It seemed almost to glow, like a real sword. "I entrust you with this sword," said the judge. "Treat it well, and use it with wisdom."

Seikei took the sword in his hands. He was almost dizzy with joy. He wanted to swing it through the air to test it, but knew that was something a boy would do in play. He acted as a samurai would, and bowed low before the judge before slipping the sword through his belt. "I am ready," he said.

Judge Ooka smiled. "We shall see."

~9~

The Road to Ise

When Seikei and the judge returned to the court-yard, two horses stood saddled and waiting. Bunzo was nowhere in sight. Seikei was glad, for the samurai could not see him struggle to get onto the horse by himself. Surprisingly, although Judge Ooka looked heavy and slow, he mounted his own horse with ease. The judge took the lead, and Seikei's horse followed.

They went out through the gate and onto the road that led east. "Aren't you going to take any guards?" asked Seikei.

"I have you," said the judge. "Won't you defend me, if we are attacked?"

"Of course, but your own men—"

"Probably you thought we would be traveling like one of those great daimyos you must have seen on the road? With dozens of samurai and servants carrying banners and loudly commanding everyone to get out of their way. Is that what you expected?"

"Perhaps not that," said Seikei. "But you are a judge, one of the shogun's own officials."

Judge Ooka nodded. "Yes, and now I am in search of a criminal. That is one of my duties. Think of it as if we were looking for a deer in a forest. Deer have sharp ears, and frighten easily. If you march through the forest with many soldiers, the deer will only run away. If you want to catch him, you must become a tree."

"A tree?"

"Yes. Deer are used to seeing trees, and have no fear of them. And a criminal will have no fear of a fat old man and a boy."

Seikei saw the wisdom of this. The road was crowded today. Even on horseback he and the judge moved slowly, for people on foot or in kagos blocked their path. Unlike Lord Hakuseki, the judge did not order people out of the way. He seemed content to move along with the crowd.

"Shouldn't we hurry a little?" asked Seikei.

"Why?"

"The thief must have left early in the morning. We are far behind him."

"But if we know where he is going, why should that bother us?" said the judge. "We will arrive in our own time."

Seikei thought about this, but could not understand. "Do we know where he is going?"

The judge nodded. "Think about the nature of the crime," he said.

Seikei thought. "A jewel was stolen. You think, then, that the thief will go someplace where he can sell it?"

Judge Ooka shook his head. "He has another purpose." Seikei tried to think of one, but could not. He followed the judge, who seemed more interested in the scenery than in looking for the thief. But why not, if he really knew where the thief was going?

Seikei decided to watch the other travelers. Among them, he saw a man wearing a dark blue robe and a basket over his head. The basket had a little slit for him to see through. He pointed the man out to Judge Ooka.

The judge nodded. "That is a *komuso*. You have not seen one before?"

"No."

"They are wandering holy men. See the flute he carries? The komusos play music to beg for food."

"Why does he hide his face under a basket?"

"That is part of the komuso tradition. They want to lose their outer selves so they can dwell on the spirit within."

Seikei shook his head. Something else for him to wonder about. "But," he said, "it would be a good disguise for a thief."

"Ah." The judge smiled. "You are right. Keep an eye on him."

Seikei felt glad to be doing something useful. But the komuso moved more quickly than they did, because he could slip easily through the throngs of people. Seikei tried to urge his horse to go faster, but it lazily continued to follow the judge's horse. And when the road turned around a hill, Seikei lost sight of the komuso. He strained his eyes, but couldn't find the bobbing basket-head in the crowd.

In places along the road, people had built little huts with straw roofs, where they sold tea, noodles, fish, pickles, and rice. The judge decided to stop at one of them. Seikei slipped down from his horse. His legs felt wobbly as he followed the judge into the hut. Inside, an old lady with gray hair stirred a large pot of miso soup.

Seikei's mouth began to water as he smelled the aroma from the pot. He realized that he had not eaten anything since breakfast. Judge Ooka placed a coin on a rough wooden table in front of the shopkeeper. She ladled noodles and broth into two bowls and set them down. Seikei finished his quickly, and the judge ordered another. "Pretty soon, you'll be as fat as me," he said.

Seikei thought it would take a long time, but said nothing. After the judge ate his noodles, he asked the shopkeeper, "Have you seen any kabuki actors on the road today?"

The old lady glanced at the two swords at the judge's belt. "So many people pass by, Lord. I don't see them all." Judge Ooka placed another coin on the table. The woman slipped it into her sleeve so quickly that if Seikei had blinked he would not have seen it.

She sucked on her teeth and cocked her head. "But early this morning something unusual happened. A group of men passed with a horse loaded with two large black trunks, like the ones actors sometimes use to carry their costumes and such. One of them wanted a bowl of noodles, but the others urged him not to stop. They wanted to go on."

"That was not unusual," murmured the judge.

She nodded and smiled, showing that she had only a few teeth. "Oh, yes, but this fellow said he had no money. He offered to do a trick for me if I gave him noodles." She put her hand over her mouth. "I cannot help laughing as I think of it. It was very funny. I let him have a bowl, for he made a face with very sad eyes. Just like an actor, you know?"

The judge nodded. "And then?"

"He took the bowl of noodles in his hand—just where you're standing now—and flipped backward, heels over head, into the road. Landed on his feet. But he didn't spill a drop of the soup! I don't know how he did it. I laughed and laughed. It was worth the soup to see that."

"Was he short?" Seikei broke in suddenly. "With a scar on his cheek, here?" He drew a line across his face.

The woman nodded and touched her cheek. "Oh, yes. Must have cut himself somehow. But he had a lovely face, even so. I never saw anybody with such beautiful eyes."

The judge thanked the woman and left her another coin. He and Seikei mounted their horses and rode on.

"Why did you ask the shopkeeper if she had seen a short man with a scar on his cheek?" the judge asked.

Seikei told the judge about the incident at the checkpoint. When the beggar stood in Lord Hakuseki's way and then flipped backward to avoid being trampled. "It seemed to me that they must be the same man," said Seikei.

Judge Ooka nodded in approval. "You are observant," he said.

"Could he be the one who stole the jewel?" asked Seikei.

The judge smiled. "Can you see a connection? Did the spirit you saw look anything like the man in the road?"

Seikei tried to remember. "I think the spirit was much taller. It had horns, and its face was very white. I didn't see any scar."

"The hallway was dark," the judge pointed out.

As they rode along, Seikei realized that only yesterday, he yearned to travel the road like this—out in the open, where he could see everything. The road wound along the seacoast here, and he looked out over the waves crashing against the stone-covered shore on his right. Seikei took a deep breath of the air, smelling the salt of the surf.

An ancient pine tree, twisted and bent by the winds, clung to a crevice in a rock at the edge of the sea. It drew Seikei's attention. He wondered how the tree managed to survive. He thought about how many people had passed by it during the years it had grown there. For some reason, it made him feel sad.

"You are thinking about that tree," said the judge.

"How did you know?" asked Seikei.

"Everyone looks at it," he replied. "Because it stands alone next to the sea. Look on the other side of the road."

Seikei looked at the hillside that rose above them. Pine trees grew all over it, one just like another.

"They are straight and tall," said the judge. "They follow their nature as trees, which is to grow, spread their branches, and in time drop their cones so that new trees will grow in their place when they die. Most people live like that, don't you agree?"

Seikei nodded. "Yet," the judge said, "everyone looks at the tree that stands alone. It is different. Fate has put it where it cannot grow straight and tall. It reminds us of something that we fear. What is that?"

Seikei thought. "I don't know," he said.

"You, a merchant's son who thinks like a samurai? You don't know? Have you ever felt that you were in the wrong place? That fate had made you different?"

"Many times," Seikei admitted softly. It was a secret thought that he had never told anyone except the girl on the terrace. He was surprised that the judge could see it so easily.

"People who feel that way sometimes become criminals," said the judge. Seikei felt guilty, as if he himself had been caught committing a crime. But the judge's smile reassured him. "Only sometimes, not always," he said. "But I think about this when I look for a criminal."

In the middle of the afternoon, they came to a fork in the road. To the right, the main road continued on to Edo. But some travelers took the smaller road that led north, away from the coast.

"They are going to Ise," said the judge. "Making the pilgrimage." Ise was the holiest place in Japan. The ancient temple there was dedicated to Amaterasu, the goddess of the sun, who was the ancestor of the first emperor of Japan. People came from all over the country to ask Amaterasu to bless their families and villages.

Judge Ooka swung his horse to the left. Seikei was surprised. "Aren't we going to Edo?" he asked.

"In time," said the judge. "We will only lose a day at Ise. Have you ever been there?"

"No," Seikei said, but he had long wanted to. It was said that a sacred mirror was kept in the temple. Indeed, it was the same mirror that the other kami used long ago to lure Amaterasu from her hiding-place. Had she not come out, the sun would never have shone on Japan. Whenever a new emperor took the throne, he came to Ise to ask Amaterasu to continue to bless Japan with her presence.

"You may be surprised," said the judge.

Seikei was. As they rode into the town of Ise, Seikei saw that it was a rowdy place. His horse was surrounded by people hawking magic charms and potions. One man shouted that his could cure any disease; another told Seikei that his would bring wealth. Seikei struggled to keep up with the judge.

Jugglers and conjurors performed their acts in the street. Seikei saw a crowd watching a trained monkey that danced and begged for coins. Young women called out to travelers, trying to get them to stop at the inns and teashops that lined the streets. One of them tried to grab the bridle of the judge's horse, but he pulled away from her. On every building, it seemed, signs proclaimed that this was the best place for food, for lodging, or for entertainment.

The judge guided his horse past all of them. Seikei expected that he would stay at the headquarters of the local government official. Again, he was wrong. The judge stopped at a stable, where he paid to have their horses fed and watered and kept for the night.

Then they walked to a back street where the houses were small and shabby-looking. Seikei was glad to be able to stretch his legs, but wondered what the judge was looking for here. A few of the houses had simple signs in front, reading TEA or RICE. None were as fancy or appealing as the shops on the main street.

"Did you keep track of that komuso we saw earlier?" the judge asked.

Seikei admitted that he had lost sight of the man.

"There he is," said the judge.

Seikei saw the komuso standing in front of one of the teahouses, playing a soft, haunting song on his flute. It did look like the same man, Seikei thought, but it was impossible to tell because of the basket on his head.

The judge walked past the komuso without looking at him, and went into the teahouse. Seikei followed, kicking off his sandals at the door. Inside, people sat at a long table, drinking cups of tea. They looked curiously at the fat samurai who had just walked in, but immediately a little man in a brown kimono appeared, carrying a tray of teacups. When he saw the judge, he put the tray down and beckoned for him to follow.

The man silently led Seikei and the judge down a narrow corridor. He slid open a door at the far end, and they went inside. The room was small and bare of any furniture except straw mats that covered the floor. The judge sat down on a mat and sighed deeply. Seikei started to ask him a question, but the judge put up his hand.

In a moment, the man returned with bowls of soup

and a pot of tea. The soup was surprisingly tasty, with pieces of green onion and tuna in it. When they had finished, the judge took his swords from his belt and laid them carefully on the mat.

"Perhaps we should get some sleep," he said. "Tonight we are going to a kabuki play."

Seikei stared. "I thought samurai were not allowed to go to kabuki theaters."

"That is true," said the judge, "but I am forced to do so as a duty to the shogun. You may enjoy it. I want you to pay close attention, so rest now."

In a moment the judge was snoring, but Seikei lay on his mat, his mind racing. He had too much to think about.

10

The forty-Seven Ronin

Seikei and the judge walked up the hill that led to the holy shrine of Ise. The judge had left his two swords behind so that he would not be known as a samurai. But he told Seikei to wear his wooden sword. "Sometimes," the judge said, "the crowds are rough, and there are pickpockets among them. I'm depending on your keen eyes and courage."

Secretly, Seikei hoped there would be no trouble. He loved to feel the sword tucked under his belt, but he had no confidence in his ability to use it.

The shrine contained many buildings. One was a monastery, where Buddhist monks spent their lives. Another building was open to travelers who could afford no other place to stay. Beyond the monastery stood the two ancient wooden shrines that were the heart of Ise. But the stream of travelers that visited them by day did not come at night, for the sun goddess slept then, and did not like to be awakened.

During the night hours, the pilgrims crowded into one of the theaters just outside the monastery grounds. Pretty paper lanterns of many colors decorated the entrances, and just as at the inns of the town, women tried to lure customers inside.

Walking from theater to theater, the judge asked what type of entertainment was being offered. One woman told him acrobats and tightrope walkers, and Seikei thought this must be the place where the thief could be found. But the judge shook his head and moved on.

At one of the theaters, they learned that a kabuki troupe was presenting the play called *The Forty-Seven Ronin*. The judge nodded and paid the price of admission for them both. When they went inside, they found that the hall was already crowded. The best seats, on the floor in front of the stage, were already taken. But there were a few places left near the two wooden runways that actors used to go to and from the stage. Seikei and the judge sat down there.

The bright lanterns hanging over the stage cast a light over the audience. People talked loudly as they waited for the fun to begin. For many of those in the audience, the trip to Ise was the most exciting thing they would ever do in their lives. People in farm villages saved money for years so that a few of them could go, and then held a drawing to choose the lucky ones. They would return and describe to the other villagers everything they had seen and done.

"I know the story of this play," said Seikei.

"Most people do," said the judge. "Yet that does not seem to lessen its popularity. Some versions of the play take three days to perform. I hope we will not be here that long. The floor is hard."

"Is it really a true story, as people say?" Seikei asked.

"Yes, and it happened not very long ago," the judge replied. "I once met a man who claimed to have known one of the *ronin*. But remember, we are here to look for a criminal who may be one of the actors. Search their faces. Try to remember if any looks like the ghost who visited your room, or even like the young acrobat you saw earlier."

"What made you choose this theater? There were acrobats performing at one of the others."

"I have a feeling that this particular story is admired by the thief. If you pay close attention, you may discover something about his character—the reason why he became a bent tree while others grew straight and tall."

Before Seikei could ask anything else, he heard the sound of two wooden blocks clapped together, the signal for the play to begin. A man ran down the wooden runway that led from the back of the theater. Suddenly he stopped and let out a wild cry—so loud that the audience hushed at once.

The actor turned and Seikei saw his face, which was

covered with white paint. But his lips were bright red and his eyes outlined in black so that everyone could see his expression. He twisted his face in fear as he called out: "Oh, what terrible things have I seen!" He looked around as if he were alone. "Who will listen? Who shall I turn to? Our lord, our daimyo is dead! What shall I do?"

Musicians hidden behind a curtain began to play. Seikei recognized the plunking strings of the *samisen,* accompanied by drums and wooden clappers. Another actor appeared on stage and called, "What has happened?" One by one, more joined him there, all wearing the two swords that marked them as samurai.

The first samurai, still out on the runway among the spectators, began to tell his story, all the while weeping, shouting, and tearing his hair. His master, the Lord of Ako, had gone to the shogun's court in Edo. As everybody knew, the shogun commanded every daimyo in Japan to live in Edo one year out of every two. That way, the shogun could keep his eye on them.

But this was the young Lord of Ako's first visit. Coming from a distant area, he did not know the correct behavior of the court. He spoke plainly and simply, not understanding when to bow and how to speak during the ceremonies.

One of the shogun's officials, Lord Kira, began to make fun of the Lord of Ako. Lord Kira called him a country bumpkin, a stupid man. The Lord of Ako ignored these insults as long as he could, but finally he heard Lord Kira question his honor.

No samurai could bear this. Although no one was permitted to wear weapons at the shogun's court, the Lord of Ako carried a dagger in his robe. He drew it and struck out at Lord Kira, wounding him.

Such an act of violence, inside the shogun's castle, was strictly forbidden. When the shogun learned of it, he commanded the Lord of Ako to commit seppuku, to kill himself. There was no other way, no appeal. The shogun's command was law. And so the Lord of Ako died by his own sword. The wooden clappers offstage sounded loudly at the story of his death. The actors on stage froze in sorrow.

"Now that our master is dead," cried the messenger, "what will become of us?" He had left Edo on horseback, riding without rest for many days to inform the other samurai of the fate of the Lord of Ako.

One of the men on stage stepped forward. Some of the people in the audience clapped, recognizing the character he played—the samurai Oishi. The actor was a short, wiry man, just like the acrobat Seikei had seen jump out of Lord Hakuseki's way on the road. Seikei stood up to see him more clearly. But because the man wore makeup it was impossible to see if he had a scar on his face.

The actor's voice rang throughout the silent theater. "We are ronin now," he said, "samurai without a master." He danced slowly down one of the runways into the middle of the theater, and the samisens played a mournful tune. "The shogun will take our lord's lands and give them to another daimyo. We can stay here to serve him. We can forget the insult that our master died for." He stopped, and turned to the others.

"Is that honorable?" His voice sounded like a clap of thunder, echoed by the drums.

Seikei could not stop himself from shouting, as many in the audience did, "No! No!"

The actor turned in a circle, staring grimly at everyone in the theater. Seikei could not tear his eyes from the man's face. "Then we must agree to give up our lives, our families, everything else that we love. We must dedicate ourselves to one thing—to avenging our master's honor, and our own!"

He ran back to the stage and then turned to face the audience. His eyes were fierce. "Do you agree?" he cried.

A great cry of "Yes!" arose. Then the Forty-Seven Ronin (there were not actually that many actors, but everyone knew how many there were supposed to be) ran off in all directions, disappearing from the stage.

Seikei felt his heart beating. He sank back onto the floor. Honor! The code that all samurai must follow, to the death. Since death came someday to all, it was more important to preserve one's honor than to save one's own life.

Yet during the next hour, each of the ronin who

had served the Lord of Ako appeared to have abandoned all thoughts of honor. It was hard to watch. Oishi himself appeared, staggering as if drunk, his clothes dirty and his hair hanging down around his face. He fell to the ground in a stupor, and passers-by kicked at him and laughed. "That pitiful creature is Oishi," they said. "He once served the Lord of Ako, but now he is a drunken fool."

Seikei squirmed, feeling the insults as keenly as the forty-seven ronin did. He watched each of the actors play the roles that the real ronin had taken. They wandered alone, spending their time in wine-shops, begging for coins, and conducting themselves in the most disgraceful ways they could think of.

The only thing that made this bearable was that Seikei knew all this was part of Oishi's plan. Finally, the last of the ronin shuffled across the stage, broken and disgraced. The lanterns overhead were snuffed out, leaving the theater in darkness. The music continued, and while the spectators waited for the next act to begin, many of them ate the food they had brought along.

But then new lanterns winked on over the stage, burning white like the light of the moon. Flakes of paper began to fall from the ceiling. It was snowing, and now the audience hushed in anticipation, for this was the wintry night when the ronin took their revenge.

One of them appeared from the shadows, clad all

in black, his two swords hanging from his belt. His step was sure and purposeful. Another arrived with a rope ladder that he threw over a wall. More ronin appeared, stealthily climbing the ladder. Others surrounded the high wall. The music grew louder, and the audience tensed.

The ronin had met, as Oishi had planned, at the castle of Lord Kira, the man who had insulted their master and caused his death. Sword fights broke out as Lord Kira's own samurai awakened and tried to fight off the intruders. Seikei gasped as the blades gleamed and clashed together. He had dreamed of taking part in such a fight, but he could not believe the skill and speed that the actors displayed. They danced across the stage, swinging their swords in a display of beauty and death.

Oishi—the actor who played Oishi—seemed to be everywhere at once, gliding as if his feet were wings, his silver sword flashing in the air. Two of Lord Kira's samurai cornered him, and pressed forward with their swords raised to kill him. Then the audience gasped as Oishi flipped backward—once, twice, three times—without dropping his sword. Then, without pausing, he turned and ran it through the two samurai who had pursued him. Seikei knew then: this must be the man he had seen defy Lord Hakuseki.

The Forty-Seven Ronin could not be defeated, and soon the floor was covered with bodies. The ronin began to search for the man they had come for—Lord

Kira. Each time they ripped aside a curtain or opened a door, the music swelled. But they could not find the lord. Children in the audience pointed to a small bamboo structure that stood at the corner of the stage. "There, look there!"

That was Lord Kira's hiding-place—an outhouse, a toilet. At last Oishi threw open the door to reveal a man dressed in a crimson robe. Oishi dragged him out, and the other ronin surrounded him, a circle of black figures with the red one at the center.

Oishi's eyes were bright with triumph. "Do you know us?" he cried. "We are the loyal men of the Lord of Ako. We suffered his disgrace at your hands. We did not forget."

He offered his own long sword to Lord Kira, holding it under his chin. "You have one chance to save your own honor. This is the sword that my lord used to kill himself. I have used it to avenge him. Take it now, take it and kill yourself, as a samurai should."

The silver blade quivered in the light. Lord Kira raised his eyes. They were filled with terror. He was, in the end, not worthy to be a samurai. He wriggled out of Oishi's grasp and opened his mouth as if to scream for help. The music rose to a high pitch, and then paused.

Before Lord Kira could utter a sound, Oishi raised the sword and in a single swift blow cut off Lord Kira's head.

The audience shrieked. The red-robed figure

slumped to the floor, and Oishi reached down and picked up the head, holding it high. For an instant, Seikei thought it was real, but then saw it was a stuffed cloth head, dripping red.

The head was swiftly placed into a basket, and the ronin marched solemnly off stage, carrying it with them.

That was not the end of the story, as Seikei knew. The music played while the lanterns were changed again, and now the ronin reappeared, bringing their basket to the court of the shogun.

The shogun was respected and feared. In him rested all the ideals of the samurai, but he ruled Japan with an iron fist. The Forty-Seven Ronin knelt before him, and once more Oishi told the story of his lord's disgrace and how he and the other ronin had avenged his honor.

The shogun, costumed splendidly in helmet and leather armor, listened in silence. When Oishi had finished his tale, the audience waited for the shogun to speak.

At last, he rose from his seat. "You have acted honorably," he said. "You have done what any samurai should do. And yet . . . I cannot allow you to kill a daimyo without punishment. I have no choice."

He bowed his head. "You know what honor demands. I release you."

One by one, the lanterns were extinguished as the shogun and his courtiers left the stage. Only the Forty-

Seven Ronin remained, standing under the single lantern that still shone.

The musicians played their terrible tune as the Forty-Seven Ronin unsheathed their swords. Many in the audience could be heard weeping, and Seikei wished silently that there could be another end to the story.

But there was not. The samurai committed seppuku, thrusting their swords into their bodies and falling lifeless upon the stage. The last to fall was Oishi himself. He turned his blazing eyes upon the audience and shouted, "Remember us! For we are the spirit of Japan!"

The last lantern went out as he used his sword on himself. For a moment, there was silence, and then the loud wooden clappers offstage began again—sounding forty-seven times. The music began again, and the lanterns winked on. The stage was empty, but the audience began to clap so loudly that the actors reappeared to bow and accept the applause.

Seikei stood to see as clearly as possible the actor who played Oishi. He was in the center of the stage, smiling and bowing. But he was too far away for Seikei to tell if he looked like the man he had seen in the Tokaido Road. "Where do the actors go after the play?" he asked Judge Ooka.

"I do not know," said the judge. "Why do you ask?"

"Let's follow them and see what that actor looks like without his makeup."

The judge yawned. "The play was a long one, and I am tired. Why don't you do it and come back and tell me what you found?"

Seikei stared. He could not understand the judge's lack of concern. Hadn't he picked out this theater himself? This might be the thief they were looking for!

Perhaps the judge was testing Seikei's courage. If so, he must prove himself. Seikei nodded and began to make his way toward the stage.

11

The floating World

Seikei found it hard to thread his way through the flow of people leaving the theater. By the time he reached the stage, it was empty. He climbed up and went behind the curtain that had concealed the musicians.

Seikei found himself in a confusing crowd of actors removing their costumes, musicians packing their instruments, and others collecting the props. He searched anxiously for the actor who played Oishi, but did not see him. One of the other actors took off his helmet and handed it casually to Seikei. Without thinking, Seikei took it.

He looked around. Another boy about his own age was packing the helmets into a chest. Seikei went over and stacked his on top.

"Not like that!" the other boy said. "I've got to fit

them all inside." He took the helmet and slipped it neatly over another one. Then he eyed Seikei.

"Who are you?" the boy asked. "I never saw you before."

"I'm looking for the actor who played Oishi," Seikei explained. "I . . . I have a message for him."

The boy snorted. "From some woman, I suppose. Well, he's gone. Didn't even take off his costume, as usual." The boy winked at Seikei. "He likes to wear it about the town, pretending he's a samurai. I'll have to go find him later to get it. Probably have to clean it too. He's likely to end up drunk."

Seikei thought for a moment. "If I help you here, will you help me find him?"

The boy shrugged. "Why not? Go pick up some of the robes. These actors will just toss them on the floor and blame me if they're wrinkled at the next performance."

As Seikei helped, he learned that the boy's name was Kazuo. He constantly complained about the actors, but it was clear that he was proud of being part of the troupe. "Are your parents actors too?" Seikei asked.

Kazuo shook his head, smiling. "Haven't got any parents," he said. "I've always lived in the kabuki. Tomomi said they found me in a trunkful of costumes when I was a baby." He shrugged. "Maybe I was a character from a play who came to life. Once in a while, they let me on stage, and I know that's where I'm des-

tined to be. Someday I want to play Oishi, when Tomomi retires."

"Tomomi? Is that the real name of the actor?" asked
Seikei.

"Tomo Tomomi he calls himself," replied Kazuo.
"But who knows what his real name is? As Tomomi
says, in kabuki anyone can become whoever he likes."

Kazuo closed the last of the chests of costumes and
locked it. Everyone else had left the theater. "You want
to go find him now?"

Seikei nodded.

"He'll likely be in the floating world somewhere,"
Kazuo said.

Seikei took a deep breath. The floating world! That
meant the houses where lanterns shone far into the
night. The pleasure quarters where beautiful *geishas*
sang and played samisens, served cups of rice wine
called *sake,* and comforted those who sought relief
from their everyday lives. Seikei's father would be hor-
rified if he knew his son was going there.

"Let's go," Seikei said.

The streets of Ise were dark and silent now. The
lines of people at the shrines would form early in the
morning, and they would be long. Most of the pilgrims had already retired to their inns or lay snoring
within the monastery grounds.

But Kazuo led him to a part of the town where the
windows still glowed and soft, enticing music tinkled
from within. The back of Seikei's head tingled as he

heard a footstep in the street behind them. He turned and saw a dark figure stepping into the shadow of an overhanging roof. Was it only his imagination, or did the figure really have a basket over its head?

"Someone's following us," Seikei whispered to Kazuo.

Kazuo looked, but the figure had disappeared. "You're just nervous," he said.

Seikei truly was nervous as they walked up to the entrance of one of the houses. He looked at its glowing paper windows and tried to imagine what lay behind them. When they stepped onto the porch, an older woman slid the door open and looked at them with disapproval.

Seikei stared at her kimono. Even in the dim light, he could see that it was made of beautiful blue silk, as fine as any he had seen on rich women in Osaka. "You boys go home to bed," she said.

"I'm with the kabuki," said Kazuo. "I'm looking for an actor."

The woman sniffed. "No actors here. This is a respectable house. Only samurai."

"He dresses like a samurai," Kazuo said. "Brown kimono with white embroidery. He has a scar on his face, right here." Kazuo drew his finger down his cheek.

"Oh," said the woman. "You mean Tomomi."

"That's right. Is he here?"

"Not tonight. I didn't know he'd returned." She

pointed down the street. "Try that place, with the green lantern in front. That's the sort of house where Tomomi would go."

This time, a younger woman opened the door. Her kimono was not as fine as the older woman's, and the hair piled up on her head was slightly out of place. She put her hand over her mouth and giggled when she saw the boys.

"We're looking for Tomomi," Kazuo said at once. "Is he here?"

She said nothing, but stood aside and pointed to the back of the house. Leaving their sandals at the entrance, Kazuo and Seikei padded across the wooden floor.

They passed several closed doors, hearing the sounds of music and laughter behind them. Seikei smelled sweet incense drifting throughout the house. Kazuo listened briefly at each door, then shook his head and moved on. Finally, they reached the last room, where a man was talking loudly. Even Seikei recognized the sound of the actor's voice. Boldly, Kazuo slid open the door and Seikei followed him inside.

Lying on a bed of many pillows was the actor Seikei now knew as Tomomi. He still wore the costume of the samurai Oishi, though his knot of hair had fallen around his head. He had loosened his obi and removed his two swords, but they lay carefully next to him, just as a samurai would have placed them.

Three young women were kneeling around him.

They were geishas, women who trained for years to please men with the arts of music and conversation. One strummed a samisen, and another was holding a tray with small cups on it. The third was rubbing Tomomi's feet.

Tomomi had been reading aloud from a book, but when the door opened, Seikei saw the man's mouth freeze and his eyes darken. Instantly he was on guard, and his hand moved a fraction toward the swords before he recognized Kazuo.

"Aha, you've found me," Tomomi said. His eyes moved to Seikei. "And who's this?" Tomomi's smile was genial, but Seikei had the feeling the man was carefully inspecting him.

"Just somebody who wants to bring you a message," said Kazuo.

Tomomi's eyes, dark and faintly menacing, went up and down Seikei. "I see he wears a sword," Tomomi said. "Come closer."

Seikei felt himself drawn forward by Tomomi's voice. Earlier, in the theater, he had felt the actor's power from a distance. Now, face-to-face, Tomomi seemed like a demon who could cast a spell over him.

"That's a beautiful piece of wood," Tomomi said, looking at Seikei's wooden sword. "Where did you get it?"

"From my lord," said Seikei, without thinking.

"And he sends you to me with a message? What is it?"

Seikei struggled to think what his answer should be. "He . . . admired your performance," he stammered.

Tomomi grinned and cocked his head. "Is that so? He sent you merely to say that? What is your master's name?"

Seikei hesitated. Should he tell the truth? The judge had not told him what to do if he found Tomomi. But Tomomi's eyes compelled him to speak.

"The samurai Judge Ooka," he said.

Tomomi threw back his head and laughed. The sound rattled through the house, shaking the paper screens that divided the rooms.

"That fat old fool," Tomomi said, wiping his eyes. "He sends a boy to find me?"

Seikei was angry and embarrassed. He let his hand drop to the hilt of his sword.

"Aha!" Tomomi said, seeing the gesture. "You will fight, then? A trained samurai, are you? Raised from birth to follow the way of the warrior?" He sat up, lazily, like a cat, and reached for one of his own swords, the long one. "Let us test each other, then."

"His sword isn't real," Kazuo murmured softly to Seikei. "Just a prop for the stage."

"Not real?" Tomomi said. "Real enough, for in a samurai's hand it can deliver a blow and draw blood." He stood up now, sword in hand, bracing his feet for combat. The three women around him gasped and drew away, looking at each other. One moved forward and put her hand on Tomomi's arm, but he shook her off.

Tomomi's eyes were taunting Seikei. "Are you willing to defend your honor?"

Seikei nodded grimly, though his hands were shaking with fear. It would be a disgrace to decline such a challenge. He drew his sword from his obi, knowing that when a samurai unsheathed his sword he must use it.

Seikei bowed, remembering the proper way of accepting a challenge to combat. "I am Seikei, the son of Konoike Toda, and a retainer of the samurai Ooka. Come take my head if you can."

Tomomi's eyes shone. "So honorable! So beautifully innocent! I feel compelled to imitate you." Then he too bowed. "I am Genji, the son of the daimyo Takezaki Kita. Descendant of a noble house, I am reduced to a homeless actor who calls himself Tomomi."

Tomomi looked around the room and his voice rose almost as if he felt himself on stage. "Yes, that is my true origin," he declared to the three women, who were cowering in a corner. Tears began to fall from Tomomi's eyes. "See me now! Disgraced, but pledged to avenge my honor." He touched his face and rubbed off the white makeup he had worn on stage.

Seikei saw the scar. Tomomi was indeed the man he had seen on the Tokaido Road, taunting Lord Hakuseki.

Tomomi traced the scar's outline on his cheek. "To

avenge this, I have pledged my life. And see—they send a boy to fight me!" Suddenly, with a loud cry, he raised his sword above his head and lunged forward.

The actor's sword whistled through the air, aimed at Seikei's head. Without thinking, Seikei raised his wooden sword to ward off the blow. The metal sword struck his—and shattered. Pieces of it flew around the room. The women shrieked and ran for the doorway.

Seikei still stood with his sword raised, not quite realizing what had happened. Tomomi looked at the shattered stump in his hand. He threw it aside and grabbed Seikei's sword with both hands. Seikei was thrown backward, but he held onto the sword with all his strength.

Yet Tomomi was much stronger. As Seikei struggled with him, he felt the man's power. He was like a demon! Tomomi wrenched the sword out of Seikei's hand, and Seikei leaped forward to take it back. As Tomomi turned aside, Seikei grabbed at the actor's robe, tearing it open.

Next to Tomomi's chest, on a silver chain around his neck, was a crossed stick with the body of a man nailed to it, arms outspread. Seikei blinked. He knew what this magic charm meant. "You are a Kirishitan!" he exclaimed.

Tomomi hastily pulled his robe together. Just then, two burly men came through the door. "No fighting!" they shouted. One of them pointed at Seikei. "You!

Out!" He picked Seikei up and slung him over his shoulder. Seikei saw Tomomi strike the other man with the wooden sword, but the blow only enraged him. He grabbed Tomomi by the scruff of his neck and shoved him out of the room.

In a few moments, the men had tossed them onto the street outside. Kazuo followed, hustling out the door on his own feet. "You're an idiot!" he shouted at Tomomi. "You broke your sword, and now I'll get blamed."

Tomomi brushed himself off. He swayed slightly, and Seikei saw that he must be drunk from the wine. "But I have another sword now. This one." He held up the wooden sword.

"That's mine," cried Seikei. "Give it back."

Tomomi grinned. "I took it from you in combat. Now it's mine. And must I remind you of the proper action for a samurai who loses his sword?"

Seikei felt his knees weaken. He knew what a disgraced samurai must do—kill himself in the ceremony known as seppuku.

He swallowed hard. "I have no sword with which to kill myself," he said. "Will you give me one?"

Tomomi laughed again, sending echoes down the dark street. He clapped Seikei on the back. "Hai! You do indeed have honor in your bones. A lesser man, not to mention a boy, would shrivel and whine that he was not a samurai at all. And you are not, are you?"

Seikei shook his head. Everyone could tell he was merely a merchant's son. "All the same, I must return my sword to my master. He entrusted it to me."

"He did well," said Tomomi. He shot a sly look at Seikei. "But before I give it to you, you must serve me. Are you willing?"

Seikei hesitated. What would the judge think when he did not return to the inn? "I will not do anything dishonorable," he said.

Tomomi nodded. "I can see you won't."

"What is it you want me to do?" asked Seikei.

"I'll let you know in the morning. Come with me now, and let us get some rest," said Tomomi. Seikei followed him and Kazuo down the street. Somewhere in the darkness behind them, he could hear the eerie sound of a flute playing.

~12~

An Offering to Amaterasu

Seikei opened his eyes and saw a man juggling swords. As they flashed through the air, he counted . . . three, four, five of them! The juggler's hands hardly seemed to move, yet he kept the swords whirling around his head in an endless circle. He glanced down at Seikei. "Awake at last, sleepyhead? I hear you were out all night with Tomomi."

Tomomi! Seikei remembered everything that had happened the night before. Tomomi had brought him back to the common hall, where pilgrims were allowed to sleep for free.

Seikei wondered what the judge must have thought when he did not return. And worse . . . Seikei felt the empty place at his side, remembering the lost sword.

He got up and looked around the large room, which consisted of little more than a roof and a floor covered by thin straw mats. A monk was distributing bowls of rice, and a few dozen men and boys were eating the simple breakfast. Seikei recognized some of them as actors who had been in the play.

The scent of the steaming rice reminded Seikei that he was hungry. But that could wait. Where was Tomomi? Where was his sword? Tomomi had promised to return it, but if he did not, Seikei could never face the judge. He was starting to compose a poem to express his misery, when someone tapped him on the shoulder.

It was Kazuo, holding out a bowl of rice and a pair of chopsticks. "I saved this for you. These greedy pigs would let their mothers go hungry if it means a full belly for them."

Seikei bowed. "I am grateful," he said. "But I must find Tomomi."

"Eat first," said Kazuo. "Tomomi went to the shrine to make an offering. But you'll never find him in the crowd. What's the rush anyway? He'll come back. We have to get on the road again. In two days, we'll be in Edo."

Seikei wanted to find Tomomi, but his growling stomach got the better of him. He took the bowl of rice and began to eat. Then he thought of something. "Why would Tomomi make an offering at the shrine?"

Kazuo shrugged. "The same reason as anybody, I guess. He wants Amaterasu's blessing."

"But he is a Kirishitan. You saw—"

"I know," said Kazuo. "He wears those crossed sticks with the man nailed onto them. That's supposed to be the Kirishitan god. I ask you, why would anyone worship a god who let himself be nailed to a cross? You know what I think?"

"What?" Seikei said between mouthfuls of rice.

"Tomomi probably wears that just because he wants to be different. The other actors are uneasy with him, even though they know he's the best actor and he writes most of our plays. He's very strange, always putting on airs. He goes off by himself to meet people in the middle of the night. But before he fought you, I never heard him say he was the son of a daimyo."

"Why would the son of a daimyo—" Seikei started to say, but then caught himself.

Kazuo nodded. "Don't worry. I know what you're thinking. What's he doing with a bunch of kabuki actors? Everybody looks down on actors, don't they?"

Seikei shook his head. "I am the son of a merchant, and everybody regards us with contempt."

"A merchant?" Kazuo looked at Seikei with interest. "In that case, why were you carrying a sword like a samurai?"

Seikei took a deep breath. He was afraid of seeming foolish, but Kazuo was so frank and open that Seikei felt he would not laugh. "My greatest dream is to be a samurai," Seikei said.

Kazuo opened his eyes wide. "Ah! That can never be. You must know that. Everyone is born into his proper place. Think of what might happen if people tried to become something they were not meant to be. There would be fighting and disorder, and everyone would suffer."

"That is what my father says," Seikei said glumly.

"If I had a father who was a merchant," said Kazuo, "I would try to please him by becoming the best merchant I could be."

Seikei remembered the judge pointing out the twisted tree on the road. The tree that grew where it could not become a proper tree. Was it meant to be a lesson for Seikei?

Seikei put down his empty bowl. "I must try to find Tomomi," he said.

"He'll return soon enough," said Kazuo. "Why go looking for trouble, when trouble will come to you?"

"Because I must recover my sword," replied Seikei.

No one stopped him as he left the hall. Outside, he found himself in the midst of a great throng of people. He saw pilgrims of every age and station in life. Some were clearly afflicted by illness, coming here to seek a cure. Mothers carried babies on their backs to present before the goddess. Old men and women were helped along by their children and grandchildren. Wealthy or poor, noble or common—it seemed as if everyone in Japan had come to beg the goddess Amaterasu for her blessing.

Kazuo was right. Seikei could not hope to find Tomomi in this mass of people. Yet he let himself be carried along as the crowed surged toward the wooden building where the spirit of Amaterasu dwelled. He could hear the sound of hundreds of hands clapping together. As the pilgrims passed through the *torii,* the great gate at the entrance to the temple area, they clapped to attract the goddess's attention.

Under the torii, Seikei clapped his hands like everyone else. Amaterasu, he prayed, help me to save my honor. Let me recover my sword.

He strained to see above the crowd. On the wooden porch of the shrine stood a group of white-robed Shinto priests. No one but them could actually go inside the shrine.

As the people passed by, the priests waved smoking sticks of incense at them. The pilgrims reached out to catch the perfumed smoke in their hands and wave it over their bodies, for it was said to cure illness. Seikei saw a mother carrying a child with no legs, trying to get close to the smoke. He could hear people in the crowd crying out with joy or weeping softly as the smoke wafted over them.

Finally his part of the crowd reached the steps of the shrine. Seikei saw large bowls there, overflowing with coins and countless other offerings that people had left. Many families had brought food that they had grown. A little girl left an onion; an aged farmer set down a gourd that grew in such an unusual shape he was convinced a kami lived within. Craftsmen offered examples of their finest work—statues of the goddess, beautifully woven mats and cloth, paper fans and umbrellas. Among the offerings was a little doll that a child must have given.

Seikei thought of Michiko, and was glad she could not see him now. Disgraced by the loss of his sword! If he could not recover it, the only honorable thing to do was kill himself. That was what a samurai would do.

Suddenly, he felt someone grasp his elbow. As he turned, he saw Tomomi's face glaring down at him. "I thought you would be here sooner," Tomomi said. "Laziness is a bad habit in one who would pretend to be a samurai."

"So is deceit," Seikei replied hotly. He pointed to his sword, hanging from Tomomi's belt. "And theft."

"No theft," said Tomomi, "I won it from you in combat."

"What about the jewel that belongs to Lord Hakuseki?" Seikei replied.

Tomomi raised his eyebrows and opened his eyes wide. "How do you know about that?" he asked in a low voice.

Seikei knew he should not have spoken of the jewel. "I . . . I was in the inn on the night it was stolen," Seikei said. "But it was found," he added hastily. "In the room of a paper-maker."

Tomomi cocked his head and looked strangely at

Seikei. "I have the feeling I have seen you somewhere else, before last night. Tell me, if the jewel was found, why did you mention it now, to me? Do you mean to accuse me of a crime I didn't commit?"

Seikei felt caught by the man's piercing eyes. He tried to think of an answer.

"No matter," Tomomi said with a shrug. "It seems that fate has brought you to see this." He reached into his robe, and drew something out of it. He held his clenched fist under Seikei's nose, and slowly unfolded his fingers.

The shining red jewel rested on his palm. Seikei gasped. Light shone from deep within it, like blood pouring out onto Tomomi's hand. It was not like glass at all. Seikei realized why people prized jewels so highly. This one must be almost as beautiful as the ancient jewel that was supposed to be kept here in the temple of Ise. That jewel was the very one Amaterasu herself had given to the first emperor long, long ago, as a sign of her blessing.

"A worthy offering for Amaterasu, don't you think?" said Tomomi.

Seikei tore his eyes away from the jewel and looked at Tomomi. What could he mean? It must be one of his cruel jests. Yet as Seikei watched, Tomomi turned and dropped the ruby into one of the offering-bowls at the foot of the temple steps. It rolled off the pile of coins and lay on the edge of the bowl.

It took a great effort for Seikei to control himself. He wanted to reach down and take the jewel back. That, of course, was unthinkable.

He turned back to Tomomi, who smiled as if he were basking in the applause of an audience. Slowly, he drew the wooden sword from his belt. "Here," he said. "You have served me, and I fulfill my part of the bargain." He turned and began to walk away.

Seikei caught him by the sleeve. "Wait. I don't understand. What did I do for you?"

"Go back and tell your master what you saw. That is enough." He shook off Seikei's hand and quickly disappeared into the crowd.

Seikei's head spun as he tucked the sword through his belt. He had discovered who the thief was, but . . . he had left the stolen jewel here. And he wanted the judge to know about it. Why? Was he trying to atone for his theft? But then why not return the jewel to its owner? Why steal it in the first place?

Seikei looked back at the ruby glittering in the sun. At the end of the day, the Shinto priests would gather it up with the other offerings. Perhaps if he could find Judge Ooka, there would still be a way to recover it.

Seikei wanted to hurry, but the crowd was so thick that it was impossible. A steady stream of people was still moving forward to the shrine. Those who had already visited it were going in the other direction, toward the sacred grove of trees. Little strips of paper fluttered from the branches of dozens of tall cedars next to the shrine. People wrote messages on these, asking for favors from Amaterasu.

Amaterasu! Seikei remembered suddenly that she had granted his wish. He turned to face the shrine again, clapping his hands. "Amaterasu," he called out. "Thank you. Thank you for helping me to save my honor."

-13-

A Hard Path to Follow

Seikei finally made his way back through the torii. He ran down the hill toward the town. The streets were unfamiliar, and it took him some time to find the one where the teahouse was. He kicked off his sandals at the entrance and ran inside.

Seikei headed for the corridor that led to the room where he and the judge had stayed. But the owner suddenly appeared and blocked his way.

"I'm staying with Judge Ooka," Seikei explained.

The man shook his head firmly. "The judge has departed. He left this for you." He held out a folded piece of paper, and Seikei opened it.

It read: "Follow the correct path."

Seikei stared at the paper, turning it over to see if it contained anything else. Nothing, not even the judge's name or seal.

"When did the judge leave?" Seikei asked the man.

"Very early," he said. "You must hurry if you want to catch up with him."

Seikei went outside and stood in the street, puzzled. Was the judge angry? Then he thought: the horses! The judge must have left Seikei's horse for him, so that he could follow.

He lost more time looking for the stables. This must be a lesson to me, he thought. I should be more observant, notice everything. With every step, he grew more worried. It was past noon now, and he had to tell the judge about the jewel before nightfall, when the gifts were taken into the temple. What could have happened to make him leave?

Finally, he found the right place. But the stable keeper shook his head. "The samurai took both horses, riding one, leading the other."

"Was he in a hurry?" Seikei asked. The man shrugged. Seikei pondered the judge's instructions. What was the correct path? It must be the highway leading to Edo. He remembered the judge telling his father that he would return Seikei safely to him there. Seikei tightened his obi and began to walk.

He kept asking himself why the judge had abandoned him. Perhaps he was angry when Seikei did not return the night before. But if he thought Seikei was in danger, why did he not look for him? Seikei began to feel resentful. Then the words of the book by the famous samurai Daidoji Yuzan sprang into his mind:

"There must be no relaxation of the duty of a warrior to respect his lord." Seikei straightened his spine and mentally apologized to Judge Ooka. He would follow the path, without question or complaint.

Later in the afternoon, he reached the fork where the road from Ise met the Tokaido Road. He turned northeast, toward Edo. There was no possibility of losing his way. The main road was filled with people going in both directions, as it always was during the day.

Seikei realized that it would take him at least two days to reach Edo on foot. Where would he stay at night? It was dangerous to sleep on the road. Bandits and robbers roamed it at night, preying on the weak and the helpless. He touched his sword. He would defend himself if attacked, but he bitterly reminded himself that last night, an actor armed only with a play sword had taken it away from him.

Seikei looked up at the sky, seeing that the sun was closer to the horizon. How far was it to the next town? He wished he had paid more attention when his father had shown him the map of the road. He studied the faces of the people he passed, looking for someone trustworthy. He saw a young couple who carried a wooden box suspended on a pole over their shoulders. It probably held wares that the couple hoped to sell.

"Excuse me," Seikei said. "Would you tell me how far it is to the next town?"

The man gave him a strange look. "Two *ri,*" he said. His wife murmured something in his ear, and he nodded. The couple began to quicken their steps, and Seikei followed after them. He wanted to find out if the town had a Buddhist temple where he could stay.

But as Seikei strode alongside, the man looked back over his shoulder. He nudged his wife and they stopped. "We must rest," the man muttered.

Seikei looked back. A gang of rough-looking carpenters were coming up behind them, their tools slung over their shoulders. The couple stood in the road until the carpenters caught up. The man said something to them, and the carpenters stared at Seikei. One of them took a heavy wooden mallet from his belt and smacked it against his palm.

"Go on, now," the carpenter said to Seikei. "You won't get anything from these good people."

Seikei was astonished. They thought he was a thief! He drew himself up with dignity. "I am in the service of the samurai Judge Ooka," he announced.

The carpenters laughed. "What would he do with the likes of you? Go find honest work, like us." They went on, leaving Seikei staring numbly at them.

He looked down at himself, realizing that his clothing was soiled and wrinkled from his encounter with Tomomi in the pleasure-house. His coat and leggings made him look like one of the masterless samurai who wandered Japan and sometimes turned to crime when they could not find a daimyo to employ them. He rubbed his face, realizing he had not washed that morning. He felt ashamed.

He trudged on. Two ri was not so far. Traveling in a kago, he and father could cover more than ten ri in a day. Father's words came back to him: "It is much safer and more comfortable to ride in a kago. If you ever had to walk any great distance, you would appreciate it more."

Well, Seikei thought, here is the chance I wanted—to see the countryside on foot. I might as well make the most of it. The road here wound through farmland, and he could see people working in the fields, their cone-shaped straw hats shielding them from the sun. It was a peaceful sight, helping Seikei to forget his troubles.

Then one of his sandals began to flop. He looked down and saw that a strap had broken. Sighing, he tried to tie it together, but he was too clumsy and his knot wouldn't hold.

He removed the other sandal and began to walk barefoot. But very soon, the rocks embedded in the road had scraped the bottoms of his feet raw. He reminded himself that a samurai will endure any hardship for his master, and forced himself to go on. Yet each step became more painful than the last, and he looked down to see that his feet were bleeding.

He sat down under a tree by the side of the road. By now the sun had set and there were fewer people on the road. He pulled up a handful of grass and wiped his feet. The grass was cool and soothing. Seikei lay back and rested his head on the ground. He couldn't get much dirtier than he was. Perhaps it wouldn't be so dangerous to sleep here. He could conceal himself in the field next to the road.

Just then, he heard the sound of a flute. He sat up and saw the basket-headed komuso approaching. Was it the same man he had seen before? It was impossible to tell. When the man reached Seikei, he stopped and looked down at him. The tune he played was lively and merry.

Seikei had the feeling that the man was mocking him. He forced himself to get on his feet again. "Who are you?" he demanded. "What do you want?"

The komuso stopped playing for a moment, and pointed down the road. Then he turned his back on Seikei and walked away. Seikei started to run after him, but his feet pained him again as soon as he touched the road.

"Why don't you help me?" Seikei called. But the komuso paid no attention.

Seikei found that he could walk slowly if he stayed in the grass alongside the road. But there were many trees there also, and walking around them made his progress slow. He heard a dog barking in the field off to his right where rows of millet were growing. Seikei realized it was coming closer. Suddenly, it jumped out of the millet field and stood in front of Seikei, barking ferociously.

Seikei froze. He took a step toward the road to go around the dog, but the animal growled and bared its teeth. Slowly, Seikei reached for his sword, wondering if he could strike the animal before it bit him. Before he drew it, however, he heard a boy's voice calling, "Inu! Inu!"

The boy appeared and threw his arm around the dog's neck. He looked anxiously at Seikei. "I apologize," he said. "Inu is trained to guard the fields. Sometimes thieves try to take our millet." He paused, and Seikei could feel the boy look at his filthy clothes. "What happened to your feet?" the boy asked. His grip on the dog seemed to loosen, and the animal responded by straining forward and growling at Seikei.

"My sandal broke," Seikei explained. He looked at the wooden clogs that the boy wore. "Would you trade your *geta* for my sandals?" he asked.

The boy looked suspicious, as if Seikei were trying to trick him. Father said that farmers thought that all people who lived in towns were thieves. This made it very difficult to buy their crops at a fair price. "My sandals are leather," Seikei said. He held the good one out to show the boy. "They're worth much more than your geta."

The boy took Seikei's sandal and examined it. He handed it back. "I would have no use for them," he said. "You could not use these for farm work. Besides," he said with a knowing smile, "you said one of them was broken."

"This is the broken one," Seikei said, showing the other sandal. "You could mend it easily. It's only the strap that's broken."

"In that case," the boy said, "why don't you fix it?"

Seikei hung his head. "Because I am too stupid to know how to tie a proper knot."

The boy laughed, and Seikei's face reddened. "Let me see it," said the boy. He patted the dog's head, saying, "Quiet, Inu," and in a moment he had tied the broken strap together. "That should hold for a while," he said as he handed the sandal back.

Seikei slipped the sandal on and tested it. It was secure. He bowed. "I am in your debt," he said, "but unfortunately I have nothing to give you."

The boy eyed Seikei's sword, obviously thinking that anyone who carried one had money as well, but he only shrugged. "You'd better hurry," he said. "There are many thieves on the road at night, and they will take your clothes and sword if you have nothing else."

Seikei needed no urging. His feet still hurt, but the sandals made it possible for him to walk faster. Even so, two ri turned out to be a greater distance on foot than in a kago. He reached the town long after darkness had fallen, but as he reached the crest of a hill, he saw the comforting lights of the inns and houses.

As he drew closer he heard the sounds of drums and gongs. A troupe of entertainers was performing in the main street. Seikei saw bright objects spinning and

113

flashing in the lantern lights. Someone was juggling swords.

Seikei moved around to the edge of the watching crowd. People were laughing and applauding. Suddenly, he felt someone clap his shoulder. "Is that really you, Seikei?"

It was Kazuo. "You look terrible," he said. "What happened to you? Tomomi wouldn't tell me. I thought you must have gone back to your master."

"I'm following the path—I mean, following my master," Seikei explained weakly. His knees trembled, and he realized that he was nearly starving. "Kazuo, please, could you give me something to eat?"

"Ha!" Kazuo snorted. "What kind of a master lets his servants go hungry? Come on, but you'll have to earn your keep if you travel with us."

-14-

A New Role

The actors had set up camp in back of a stable, for this small town had no temple offering shelter. Everyone shared a large pot of warm rice and sea bream. Seikei thought it was the best meal he had ever eaten. As soon as his bowl was empty, he lay back and listened to the actors talking and singing. He looked up and saw the stars overhead. Then his eyes closed, and the next thing he knew Kazuo was shaking him.

The stars had disappeared and the sky was now streaked pink from the rising sun. Though Seikei's feet still pained him and his legs were stiff, he followed Kazuo to a nearby stream. Kazuo stripped off his clothes and jumped into the water. Seikei quickly joined him. The stream was freezing cold, but he washed off the dust of the road with relief.

Kazuo rinsed some of the actors' costumes in the

water and spread them on rocks to dry. "This town is too small to make it worthwhile to put on a play," he explained. "We're just picking up a few coins by performing tricks and such. But in a few days we'll be in Edo, and the *bon* festival will be starting. Tomomi says he'll have a brand-new play for us to perform."

"He's writing it?" said Seikei.

"He writes all our plays. The most popular one is *The Forty-Seven Ronin,* of course. Many kabuki troupes perform some version of that story. But Tomomi's is best, don't you think?"

"It's the best one I've ever seen," Seikei said. He didn't mention it was the only one he'd seen. "What is the new play about?"

"Tomomi won't tell anyone yet. He likes surprises. He's been rehearsing the actors separately, so that nobody knows the whole play. Of course, he'll give himself the main role. He always does."

Seikei clambered out of the water and dried himself. As he put on his clothes, Kazuo said, "I see you got your sword back. What did you have to do for it?"

Seikei hesitated. How much did Kazuo know about the theft of the ruby? "I watched him make an offering at the shrine of Amaterasu," he explained.

Kazuo gave him a skeptical look. "Is that all?"

Seikei shrugged.

"Well, maybe he wanted to prove he wasn't a Kirishitan," Kazuo suggested. "Is that why this judge, your master, has his eye on Tomomi?"

The question made Seikei uncomfortable. He remembered the reason why Judge Ooka had told him to investigate Tomomi—to see why he became a bent tree. "No," he said. He looked at Kazuo, and decided that he was so open and honest that he could not possibly have anything to do with the theft.

"Were you with Tomomi at the checkpoint outside the town of Kameyama?" Seikei asked. "Did you see what he did?"

Kazuo wrinkled his brow. "Kameyama? How many days ago was that?"

Seikei counted. "Three." Was it only three days ago? So much seemed to have happened since then.

"Oh, I remember," said Kazuo. "Tomomi was in one of his crazy moods. He pretended to be a beggar, and stood in front of a daimyo's procession. We were all terrified, because we thought he'd lose his head for sure."

"That was it," said Seikei. "What happened that night, in the town? Do you remember? Was there anything strange?"

"Let's see. We put on a love-suicide play. You know, one of those where two people are in love but their families forbid them to marry, so they kill themselves. I can never understand why they don't just agree to marry the people their families picked out for them. Do you?"

"But afterward," urged Seikei. "What happened after the play?"

"Well, we slept in the Buddhist monastery. We had a good meal too. Lots of shrimp, because some boatman had donated so much to the monastery that the monks distributed it to the travelers."

"I mean Tomomi. What did he do?"

Kazuo shrugged, and put his finger to his nose. "I remember. He went to see a friend of his—he knows lots of people along the road—and he wore his costume as usual, but when he came back, it was covered with mud. I thought it was ruined, but I managed to clean it off. Good thing too. He plans to use it in the new play."

Covered with mud, thought Seikei. He remembered his trip through the tunnel underneath the inn. It was almost certain that Tomomi had taken the jewel. But why, if his intention was only to offer it at the Ise shrine? Seikei wished he could find the judge and tell him what he'd discovered.

When the costumes were dry, Seikei helped Kazuo fold them neatly. They returned to the actors, who were preparing to leave. Tomomi spotted Seikei and walked over. "I thought I told you to return to your master," he said. "Did you tell him what you saw?"

Seikei shook his head. "He has gone on without me," he confessed. "May I travel with you?"

Tomomi laughed. "Why not? Kazuo needs a helper, and perhaps we can find some other use for you."

Seikei wondered uneasily what that might be.

Kazuo gave him some straw sandals that were better

for walking, and as the sun rose higher in the sky Seikei's stiffness soon wore off. Traveling with the troupe made the journey easier. The actors had one old horse that they loaded with the trunks that held their props and costumes. As they marched along, they passed the time by singing, telling jokes, and practicing scenes from their plays.

At midday, they came upon one of the food stands that dotted the road. Tomomi offered to pay for their meal by displaying his acrobatic skill. The man who owned the stand shook his head. "I've seen enough acrobats," he said. "Dozens of them have passed by on their way to Edo these past few days."

"How about a sword fight?" Tomomi suggested.

The man's eyes lit up. "That would be good to see," he said.

Tomomi nodded to Kazuo, who quickly opened the box that held the swords. Tomomi handed them out to several of the other actors. "Now," he said to the owner of the stand, "these five men will be your loyal samurai. They will defend you against my attack. But if I fight my way through, you will serve us soup."

The man laughed. "They will allow you to win."

Tomomi bowed. "You will be the judge of that."

The five actors grouped themselves in a semicircle in front of the food stand. Tomomi stepped back into the road, a long sword in his right hand and a short one in his left. Suddenly, he leaped forward, and the five actors closed around him. Their swords cut through the air, but Tomomi parried every thrust. He danced backward and to the side, stabbing out with the short sword to strike down a man who came too close. The actor fell to the ground with a cry, and the other four circled Tomomi warily.

Seikei watched in fascination. He had seen Tomomi's skill on stage during the performance of *The Forty-Seven Ronin,* but up close the actor was even more amazing. Every step he took was swift and sure, like a dancer's. All the while, his hands moved with grace and speed, now defending, now attacking. His swords whistled through the air, cutting down a second man, and then another.

Seikei forgot that it was only play-acting, for the cries of the men who fell seemed real. Tomomi's last two opponents split up, and approached him cautiously from either side. It seemed certain that one of them would strike Tomomi. But as they rushed him, he ducked low to the ground, dodging both sword thrusts, and then rose and whirled in a single movement. His two swords struck both his opponents' necks at the same time.

Triumphant, Tomomi's eyes blazed like a wild man's. Now he danced toward the owner of the stand, holding his long sword at arm's length. He touched the side of the owner's neck with the blade, and the man's eyes bugged out. "Your head?" Tomomi said. "Or the soup? Do you keep your promise?"

"Yes, Lord," the man whispered, and the actors rose

from the ground like men coming back from the dead. The owner rushed to fill bowls for them.

Tomomi casually handed his swords to Seikei. "Collect the rest of the swords and put them away," he said, "and you can eat too."

When they set out on the road again, Seikei walked alongside Tomomi. "It is true, then. You really are a samurai, aren't you?" he said.

Tomomi turned his head slightly. "Just an actor," he replied.

"Who then is Genji, the son of Takezaki Kita?"

Tomomi glanced sharply at him. "Who told you that name?"

"You did," said Seikei. "In the floating world."

"I must have been drunk," said Tomomi. "Forget that name. It was a character from a play."

"Only a man born to be a samurai could display your skill with a sword," Seikei said.

"Do not think so," Tomomi said, shaking his head. "Nothing about birth qualifies a man to use a sword—merely the shogun's order that samurai alone may carry them. Skill with a sword is like juggling or playing an instrument. A man learns it through practice." Tomomi gave Seikei a sly look. "I can teach you."

The hair on the back of Seikei's neck stood up. He reminded himself to be wary. "What would I have to do in return?" he said.

"Nothing much. Perhaps take a role in a play I am writing," Tomomi said.

Seikei took a deep breath. "You mean act? On stage?"

"It will not be in a theater, nor will the audience be very large," said Tomomi. "You will not find it difficult."

Seikei hesitated, trying to think. The judge had told him to become a tree to catch the thief. Now Seikei knew the thief was standing before him. It seemed the correct path was to become an actor so that he would win Tomomi's trust. "I agree," he said.

-15-
Under the Komuso's Mask

As they drew closer to Edo, the number of checkpoints increased. Mostly, however, the guards were examining those who traveled in the other direction. One of the ways the shogun kept his control over the country was by commanding the daimyos and their families to spend every other year in Edo. Though the lords were treated as the "guests" of the shogun, they were really hostages—guarantees that no daimyo would raise an army of samurai to rebel against the government. The checkpoints outside Edo were set up to prevent any of the wives or children of the daimyos from slipping out of the city without permission.

In the afternoon, as the actors were waiting in line at a checkpoint, rain began to fall. Many people in the line unfurled oil-paper umbrellas whose colors made them look like flowers blooming in the spring. But the actors' only umbrellas were the ones they used on stage, and they were too delicate to use in a real rainstorm.

The line moved slowly, and Seikei's clothing was soon soaked through. It stuck to his skin, chilling him. He thought again of the kago, where he would have been sheltered and dry.

That didn't matter, he told himself. A samurai must be willing to endure any hardship, and a little rain was nothing. His master, Judge Ooka, had told him to follow the correct path. Seikei had indeed found the thief the judge was seeking, but now Seikei depended on the charity of the thief to survive. Perhaps, he thought gloomily, he would never see either the judge or his father again.

He gritted his teeth and forced such thoughts out of his mind. Follow the path, he told himself again. But was this really the right path?

Late in the day, they trudged down the steep mountain road that led to the town of Hakone on the shore of Lake Ashi. The sunset over the lake, seen from here, was famous for its beauty, but Seikei could see nothing but slate gray clouds that grew steadily darker. The scene matched his mood.

In Hakone they found a theater whose owner willingly invited the troupe to put on a play. Tomomi led the others inside. "We have little time to prepare," said Tomomi. "So we will present a simple drama, one that always proves popular. Get out the costumes for the love-suicide play."

While the actors prepared, Seikei and Kazuo were sent to spread word of the performance and draw people to the theater. Kazuo told Seikei to visit the inns along one side of the street while he took the other. "What am I supposed to do?" Seikei asked.

"Tell everyone you see that there will be a performance of *The Double Suicide at Sonezaki* at the theater. It's a famous play. Even the farmers come to see it. Sneak inside the door of the inn and shout it in the hallway."

"Won't that disturb the guests?"

Kazuo shook his head impatiently. "Who cares? They won't do anything but throw you out. Just make sure everybody hears you."

Seikei approached the first inn shyly. Two pretty young women stood outside, trying to entice travelers inside. Seikei realized his task was similar to theirs, and remembered that his father always said inns that used such methods were inferior.

The women paid no attention as he slipped by them. But at the top of the steps he found his path blocked by a burly innkeeper. "Do you wish to stay here?" the man asked.

"There is a play," Seikei replied. He tried to raise his voice so that it would carry inside. "The . . . the *Double Love of Sonezaki*. I mean *Suicide*. At the theater. Down the street." He could not make himself shout, and he realized that no one but the innkeeper could possibly hear him.

The man pushed Seikei down the steps, nearly causing him to fall. "Go away," he said.

"The Double Suicide!" Seikei cried, a little louder this time because he was angry. "Come see!"

The innkeeper threw a stone at him. As Seikei fled past the two women, he realized that their voices were louder than his.

Glumly, he walked to the next inn. This one had no women in front. It looked a bit more elegant than the first one. Seikei was certain he would be thrown out as soon as he entered the door.

He hunched his shoulders and walked up the steps. Before he reached the door, it opened. A komuso stood there, like the other one, wearing a basket over his head. Seikei wondered again if this was the same komuso he had seen earlier.

The komuso raised his hand and gestured for Seikei to come inside. Seikei took a step backward, suspicious. He decided it would be just as well to go on to the next inn. As he turned, however, the man swept forward like a demon. He picked Seikei off the ground and tossed him over his shoulder as easily as if he had been a sack of rice.

Seikei struggled, but it was useless against the man's strength. As they moved through the doorway, Seikei caught sight of Kazuo entering a teahouse across the street. Seikei started to cry for help, but the komuso clapped a hand across his mouth.

The main hall of the inn was deserted. No one noticed as the komuso carried Seikei down a hallway. He slid open a door and plopped Seikei down on the floor. At once, Seikei jumped to his feet and reached for his sword, determined to give the komuso a fight.

"Hold!" came a loud voice. Seikei recognized it, and froze. He turned to face Judge Ooka, who was sitting calmly on a mat, a steaming pot of tea by his side. Seikei could not keep himself from staring.

"I thought you knew that a samurai only draws his sword in order to use it," the judge said sternly.

"I intended to use it," Seikei replied. He turned and pointed to the komuso. "This man meant to rob me."

"Nonsense," said the judge. "You have nothing for him to steal. Why not be patient and see where he was taking you? You owe him an apology. Kneel now and beg his forgiveness."

Seikei hesitated only for a second. He knew he had to obey his lord without question. He knelt on the floor before the komuso. "I beg your forgiveness," he said, bowing his head.

The judge clapped once. "You are acquiring discipline," he said. "Now look at the man I sent to protect you."

When Seikei looked up, he saw that the komuso

had removed the basket from his head. It was Bunzo, the samurai who had showed him how to ride a horse.

Seikei's astonishment showed on his face, and Bunzo grinned. "I told the judge how you continued on the road even though your feet were bleeding."

"And much else," the judge added. "Now I must hear what you have seen. Be quick, for I think we must soon part again."

Seikei began to pour out the story of everything he had seen since he left the judge at the theater. He bowed his head in shame when he revealed that the actor had taken his sword, but the judge stopped him. "Tell me again the name he gave when you fought."

"Genji, the son of the daimyo Takezaki Kita."

"Takezaki Kita," the judge repeated slowly. "A Kirishitan daimyo, who was executed when he refused to give up his faith."

"Tomomi—or Genji—himself wears the cross of the Kirishitans around his neck," Seikei said. "But I must tell you the rest. I know he stole the jewel, for I saw him with it the next morning at the shrine of Ise. He left it there as an offering to Amaterasu!"

"Of course," the judge said. "What else would he do with it? It would be impossible to sell it."

Seikei was disappointed that his report caused so little surprise. "He told me to tell you what I had seen," Seikei said.

The judge nodded. He took a sip of his tea. "The fact that he wishes it known is significant. I think I see where his path will lead him." He wagged a finger at Seikei. "But he must not know you have told me already," he said. "Then he might change his plans. Go back to him now and do what he says."

"Go back?" said Seikei. "But you know he is the thief. You know where the jewel is. Shouldn't you—" he caught himself in time. It would be wrong to tell the judge his duty.

"The jewel is perfectly safe," the judge said. "We must let Genji follow his own path. He has another performance in his mind."

"That's true," said Seikei. "They say he is working on a new play."

"Is that so?" said the judge. "Then I must be there to see it. There may be another criminal in the case. Genji will show me who it is." The judge folded his hands across his stomach. "I am pleased that he trusts me so much."

Seikei had a thousand questions, but the judge urged him to hurry. "There will be time later to examine the case in detail. Do whatever Genji tells you. Find out whatever you can about him. Bunzo will follow you as before, and keep me informed of your progress." Judge Ooka smiled. "You have proved resourceful, a desirable quality in a samurai."

Seikei silently glowed with pleasure as he bowed to the judge and left the room. As he hurried down the hall, he reached down and touched his wooden sword. For the first time, he felt worthy of wearing it. It did not matter that he had lost it once. He had pleased the judge.

I must continue to be resourceful, Seikei told himself. Do what Genji says. The trouble was, he didn't have the slightest idea what Genji wanted him to do. He shrugged. The judge seemed to understand. All Seikei had to do was continue to follow the path, wherever it led.

16

The Magic of Kabuki

As Seikei stepped outside the inn, he found Kazuo waiting for him in the street. "What were you doing so long in there?" Kazuo asked.

"Telling the guests about the play." Seikei responded quickly.

Kazuo looked at him suspiciously. "I guess they didn't throw you out because you're wearing a sword," he said.

"The innkeeper wasn't around," Seikei explained.

"Dumb luck," muttered Kazuo. "At one of the teahouses, they threw boiling water at me." He shrugged. "Let's get back to the theater. There's work to do."

When they arrived, Seikei saw a scene of bewildering confusion. People were rushing about—some partly dressed in costumes, some setting up lights for the stage, some carrying tea utensils, paper screens, and other props. A group of musicians sat off to one side, playing their instruments and shouting at each other at the same time. Three of the actors, spotting Kazuo, yelled at him at once. "Where's the scarlet makeup?" "What happened to the sandals for my costume?" "Find me a mirror!"

As Kazuo rushed off on three errands at once, Seikei wandered through the backstage area, trying not to bump into anyone. He felt a hand grab his sleeve. Seikei turned and nearly jumped at the sight of a fierce chalk-white face, with crimson and black lines around the eyes. "Get me a sword!" When Seikei hesitated, the actor pointed to a chest on the other side of the room. "The green chest. Get the sword with the plain black scabbard."

Hurrying through the crowd, Seikei opened the green chest. It was filled with swords, daggers, spears, bows and arrows, bottles of poison—a treasure trove of deadly objects. As he examined them, however, he saw that they were only props. He slipped one of the swords from its scabbard and cautiously rubbed his thumb along the edge. It was as dull as the edge of a plate. A good thing, for as he knew, a real samurai sword was razor sharp and strong enough to cut a man's body in two with a single blow.

He selected the proper sword and took it back to the actor. The man slipped it through the sash of his kimono and stood with his arms stretched out. The kimono was made from a deep purple cloth covered with silver and gold embroidered animals. The wide sleeves fluttered gracefully as the actor turned. "What do you think?" he asked Seikei.

"It's . . . amazing," said Seikei. Suddenly, the actor whipped the sword from its scabbard and raised it high. Seikei ducked instinctively, and the man laughed. "You'll see that move again when I strike off Tomomi's head," he said.

Seikei looked around. "Where is Tomomi?" he asked.

"Oh, he thinks he's too good to dress with the rest of us," the actor said. "He's hiding behind a screen somewhere, changing himself into a woman."

"A woman?" said Seikei. "How can he do that?"

"The magic of kabuki," the actor replied. "Don't you know that the shogun forbids women from appearing on the stage?"

"Oh . . . I think I did hear that," said Seikei.

"A pity, for it was a woman, the immortal Okuni, who invented kabuki." He gave Seikei a wink. "But it is all in the same spirit, for Okuni took men's roles. In kabuki, you see, you can never tell what's real."

That was true enough, thought Seikei. He looked around, seeing the ordinary-looking men transforming themselves into strange and spectacular figures. One actor's kimono was so immense that it made him look as broad as he was tall. In fact, two assistants crouched behind him, holding thin sticks that supported the sides of the kimono. The three of them practiced now, stepping in unison so that the audience would not see the assistants.

The backstage confusion seemed to increase as the time of the play grew near. Seikei looked for a place where he could watch everything and not be in the way. Shyly, he followed the musicians. They took their places behind a platform where they could see the action on stage. Still arguing among themselves, they paid no attention to Seikei.

All at once, the argument stopped. The musicians looked toward the back of the theater. There, Seikei saw the actor wearing the purple kimono raise his hand. As he jumped onto the runway, one of the musicians picked up two thick wooden blocks. He clapped them twice, so loudly that Seikei put his hands over his ears. The actor began to run toward the stage. Drums rolled, bells tinkled, and the samisens played a lively tune. The play was on!

The story was not hard to follow. The actor in the purple kimono was Toshio, the son of a rich merchant. Seikei suddenly grew more interested. Toshio complained to the audience that his parents had chosen a bride for him, but he loved another.

In the first scene, Toshio's father—the actor with the very wide kimono—waddled on stage. People in the audience jeered. He did look ridiculous, like an immensely fat man who had made a fortune off others. A typical merchant, thought Seikei ruefully.

For his son's bride, Toshio's father had chosen the

daughter of another merchant. The father described the benefits of two great merchant houses uniting through this marriage. Toshio protested, but to no avail. His father's word, like the shogun's, was law. His children had to obey his wishes in all things.

The bride's father and brother came to meet Toshio. The audience laughed as they sternly questioned the young man. He tried to make himself appear stupid, but they were pleased by his modesty. He confessed that he did not have a great liking for girls, but the relatives reassured him—the bride didn't like men either.

From the standpoint of Toshio's family, the important thing was that the bride was obedient. When the marriage took place, she would come to live in Toshio's parents' house. She would serve his parents as if she were their own daughter. The happiness of the bride and groom was of little importance. In time, they would have children to carry on the family name—and the business. The relatives departed, bowing deeply to Toshio and his father, who returned the gesture. The prospective groom had been accepted. No one except the audience saw Toshio's misery.

Toshio's family unfolded their tatami mats and settled in for the night. But after everyone else was asleep, Toshio sneaked away. The stage darkened, and the stage crew swiftly set up a new scene. As the lanterns lit up again, the audience saw a teahouse in the "floating world." The silhouette of a beautiful geisha was reflected onto a paper screen. Softly she played the samisen and sang a mournful song, lamenting her lover who had failed to come to her tonight.

Seikei sat up abruptly, mouth open, staring at the screen with the shadow-image of the geisha. That was exactly what he had seen on the screen of his room in the Tokaido Inn. What he had imagined were the horns of the jikininki were actually the pins that the geisha stuck in her thick hair. This was the ghost.

Toshio appeared out of the darkness and came tiptoeing up to the teahouse. He tapped twice on the screen. A high voice—exactly like a woman's—called out, "Who is there?"

"It is Toshio. I have come. Please, I must see you."

Fascinated, Seikei could not tear his eyes away as the screen slowly slid open, revealing a beautiful geisha clad in a blue kimono covered with embroidered white chrysanthemums. The audience broke into applause. They knew it must be a man, and appreciated the illusion he created.

It was impossible to tell that the actor was not a woman. It was not just the kimono, the makeup, and the wig. Every step and gesture was delicate and alluring. Seikei half fell in love with her himself, till he reminded himself that this was in fact the man he knew as a thief—Tomomi. Or was he really Genji, the son of a samurai? Clearly, he could be anyone he wished to be. For a second, Seikei envied him, understanding why a man would wish to be something he was not. But why would anyone give up being a samurai? That would be the greatest disgrace of all.

Seikei sat mulling over his thoughts as the play continued. On stage, Toshio pledged his love to the geisha, whose name was Motoko. As he told her of the marriage his father had arranged, she knelt before him and grasped his hands. "Will you still think of me when you are married?" she asked.

"Think of you?" Toshio cried. "It would be impossible for me to live without you. I cannot think, I cannot eat, I cannot sleep in my distress. Tonight I came here because I want you to run away with me."

Motoko's hands fluttered like swans. "There is no place where we can go," she said.

"There is! There is!" Toshio insisted. "We can travel to the north, find some place where no one knows us."

Motoko shook her head and turned away from him. "I cannot go," she said with a sob. "I am bound here for twenty years, obliged to serve the teahouse until the end of that time."

"That doesn't matter!" cried Toshio. "The teahouse owner will never find us, I promise you. We will go to the other side of Fujiyama, to a fishing village on the coast."

"And how will we live?" asked Motoko, turning toward him with a sad smile.

"I will become a fisherman," he said, nodding earnestly. "Every day I will cast my nets into the sea and bring up so many fish"—Toshio spread his arms wide, trying to carry all the imaginary fish—"that we will soon become rich."

The wistul look on Motoko's face showed that she knew it was only a dream. "I cannot leave the teahouse," she said softly. "My parents, who are old and frail, received a payment for sending me to work here. In return, I promised to stay for twenty years. If I left, my family would be dishonored."

Seikei, and everyone in the audience, knew that this was a powerful reason. From their earliest childhood, everyone was taught the importance of family. Just as it was unthinkable for Toshio to refuse his father's choice of a bride, so it was impossible for Motoko to disgrace her parents by breaking her contract.

Toshio and Motoko danced and sang to express their love and pain. They yearned for nothing more than to remain together, but as the sun rose, Toshio tore himself away while Motoko sank to the floor in tears.

Toshio walked along the narrow runway that extended out into the audience. Lamenting his fate, he cried, "What to do, what to do? I must find a way to rescue Motoko so that we can be happy. But how?"

Just as he asked this question, there was a jangling sound offstage. The musicians added the sounds of their instruments to it, and as the jangling grew louder, Toshio's eyes opened wide. Everyone in the audience could see that he was struck by a great idea. The jangling was the sound of money.

As Toshio crept closer to the stage, a screen slid aside so that the audience could see his father counting his money. Seikei's face burned at the sight. The grossly fat merchant was sitting at a table that held endless stacks of glittering coins—silver, gold, copper. The old man's face showed the delight he felt in his wealth. But as his son Toshio walked slowly around the table, the audience had the same thought Seikei did—he had so much, he wouldn't miss some of it.

17

The Double Suicide

It made Seikei feel uneasy to watch Toshio carefully lay plans to steal his father's money. Seikei could not help recalling the strongbox at home where his own father kept the profits from his business. The play's message seemed to be that disgracing one's family was forbidden, but stealing from one's father was all right—as long as he was only a merchant.

Unhappily, Seikei got up and walked backstage. Most of the actors were preparing for the next scene, which was to be Toshio's wedding to the merchant's daughter. Seikei looked around for Tomomi, wanting to see the actor up close in his female costume. He seemed to have disappeared, and Seikei cautiously approached the screen behind which the actor had prepared for his role.

Tomomi wasn't there either, but Seikei noticed that

a large trunk had been left open. It was overflowing with costumes—gorgeous silk kimonos of crimson, sky blue and forest green. Seikei lifted one of them carefully, letting the silk run through his fingers like water. As he placed it back in the trunk, his fingers touched something hard underneath the costumes.

Curious, he reached down and felt the hilt of a sword. Seikei looked over his shoulder, checking to see if anyone was watching. Slowly, he lifted the sword. It was sheathed inside a scabbard made of black lacquer that shone so brightly Seikei could see the shadow of his hand pass over it. Set into the surface of the lacquer were silver crosses—the Kirishitan kind, with one arm longer than the other three. Seikei was certain that this was not a prop—it was a real sword.

The voices from the room on the other side of the screen had died down. The cast had gone on stage for the big wedding scene, and Seikei could hear the muffled sounds of the music starting. Cautiously, he wrapped his hand around the hilt, which was wrapped with silver threads to make it easier to grasp. The sword slid out noiselessly, with just the slightest resistance—as it should, for it was meant to serve its owner as easily as if it were a part of his body.

Respectfully, Seikei exposed only a few inches of the blade. His heart pounded when he saw its polished surface, which gleamed like a mirror. There was no doubt that this was a sword that a master craftsman had forged, perhaps centuries ago. Such objects were passed down from samurai to samurai for generations. Seikei knew that if he touched the edge with his thumb, it would draw blood. The men who made such swords tested them on the bodies of executed criminals—if a blade could not cut through a corpse with a single blow, it was melted down.

The rustle of a silk kimono made Seikei jump. As he turned his head, he found himself staring into the face of the geisha Motoko. The illusion was so complete that it took a second before Seikei realized who it really was—and then he remembered to be afraid.

Seikei stammered an apology as he slid the sword carefully back in the scabbard, but Motoko seemed not to notice. Her eyes remained as gentle and sad as they had been on stage. "What do you think of my son's sword?" she said.

Seikei was wary. The voice was that of a young woman's, not of a man's. He knew this was really Tomomi, but Tomomi refused to step out of his role.

"I didn't—I didn't know you had a son," Seikei replied to the geisha's question.

Swift as a cat, she reached out and cupped Seikei's chin before he could draw away. He could feel her long nails press into the flesh of his neck. "Oh yes, yes, I have a son," she said with a sad smile. "You look a bit like him, in fact. His name was Genji, but now he calls himself Tomomi." Her dreamlike eyes probed into his, and Seikei felt that he was looking into a woman's soul. "Do you know why he had to change his name?" Motoko asked.

The question, and the eerie voice in which it was asked, made Seikei very uncomfortable. It seemed almost as if she really thought they were talking about someone else. "No I don't," said Seikei. "Why?"

"Because of me," she replied.

Seikei twisted his head to slip out of her grasp. Just at that moment, Kazuo put his head around the corner of the screen. "Oh, there you are. It's time for your suicide, Tomomi."

The actor's eyes cleared briefly, and he nodded, waving Kazuo away. Then he became Motoko again, softly placing an arm around Seikei's shoulders. "Come watch," she said. "I want you to see, to remember how it is done."

Reluctantly, Seikei followed and took his place with the musicians again. As the play unfolded to its tragic climax, the audience saw Toshio's plans unravel. Though he had bought Motoko's freedom from the teahouse with the stolen money, his theft had been discovered. Toshio's father, enraged when his son did not show up for the wedding to the merchant's daughter, reported his son's crime to the local judge, who sent samurai to find the fleeing couple.

The play's final scene took place on a cliff overlooking a rushing river. Toshio and Motoko were trapped, but they sang to each other, describing how they would meet again in another world, reborn into new bodies in a place where they could find happiness. They turned toward the audience one last time, begging them to remember the story of two people whose only crime was that they loved each other. Linking arms, they leaped over the cliff together as the music swelled to a crescendo.

The audience applauded wildly. Seikei looked across the stage at Kazuo, who was standing behind the scenery with bamboo whisks that imitated the sound of flowing water. Kazuo shrugged, as if to say, "Who knows why people like suicides so much?"

But Seikei understood. It was the only honorable thing to do. By choosing to die, Toshio and Motoko showed that their love for each other was stronger than the fear of death.

As Seikei was meditating on this, he felt a hand grasp his arm, and turned to see once more the face of the geisha, who had risen from her watery grave to come up behind him. But now, even with her makeup, she was again Tomomi. "You remind me of myself when I was your age," he whispered. "You must stay with me. I have much to teach you."

That very night, Seikei's training began. Tomomi kept him at the theater after the other actors had removed their makeup and costumes and departed. Tomomi seemed to have completely forgotten finding Seikei searching through his trunk. "In Edo," he said while removing his makeup and costume, "I am going to present a new play. You will have a role in it."

"But I am not an actor," Seikei protested. "Use Kazuo. He wants to appear on stage."

Tomomi waved the suggestion away. "The role is that of a son of a samurai. Kazuo has no talent for it." He pointed at Seikei's wooden sword. "Why are you wearing that? What does it signify?"

Seikei took a deep breath. "I am not really a samurai. I am only a merchant's son."

Tomomi shrugged. "So you are playing a role already. Continuing it on stage will not be difficult." He smiled. "I told you I could teach you to use a sword. Are you ready?"

Seikei could not resist. It was the chance to learn from a master. For hours they practiced in the empty theater with the dull swords that the kabuki troupe used. Tomomi taught Seikei how to move his feet swiftly, sliding not stepping, never crossing one foot over the other, moving back and forth and side to side, as easily as if he were a dragonfly on water.

At last Tomomi nodded. "You can imitate the footwork, but of course you are holding the sword completely wrong." He replaced his own sword in the scabbard, and then drew it again with a flash. "One hand brings out the sword," he said. "But then you must seize it with both hands. Like this."

Seikei followed his example, finding that the hilt of the sword was long enough for both of his hands.

"Raise it! Raise it!" Tomomi commanded, and Seikei lifted it high over his head.

"That's right," Tomomi said, and without warning slapped his own sword across Seikei's cheek. Stung by the blow, Seikei rushed forward, trying to return it.

But the actor stepped aside, tripping Seikei as he went by and sending him sprawling to the floor. Tears rushed to Seikei's eyes, but he was determined not to let Tomomi see them.

"What do you say? What do you say?" Tomomi shouted.

Seikei stared at him, open-mouthed. He did not know what a samurai said when humiliated. "Must I kill myself?" he asked.

"You say," Tomomi replied slowly, "I swear that I will see you disgraced."

Silence fell over the room. "Say it!" Tomomi commanded.

"I swear," Seikei repeated, "that I will see you disgraced."

"That will be your most important line in the play," Tomomi said. "Always watch your opponent's eyes," he added casually. "And now to bed. Tomorrow we must reach Edo."

-18-

A Sword Fight

Tired as he was, Seikei got little sleep that night. Dreams of what he had learned kept waking him. The image of Tomomi dressed as the geisha burned in his memory. If he needed any further proof that Tomomi had stolen the jewel, that provided it. Now Seikei knew that it was Tomomi, wearing that same costume, who had appeared in the doorway of the room in the Tokaido Inn. Because Seikei had just heard the story of the horned jikininki, he had imagined that was what it was.

Seikei could hear his father's voice scolding him for having too much imagination. Somehow, Judge Ooka had guessed the truth, connecting Seikei's story to the troupe of actors who had performed nearby. But the mystery only seemed to deepen, for why would Tomomi go to such trouble to steal the jewel and throw blame on someone else by leaving a false one—and then leave it at the shrine of Ise?

The answer must be revealed in his new play. Judge Ooka had thought so. "There may be another criminal," he had said. Who could that be?

Most of all, Seikei's dreams were haunted by the sword, the real sword, in Tomomi's trunk, and the actor's strange reaction when he discovered Seikei handling it. Anyone else would have been enraged. But over and over, Seikei heard the woman's voice— the geisha who had ceased to be Tomomi—asking, "What do you think of my son's sword?" The sword, sharp and shining and deadly, flashed toward Seikei in his dreams.

Seikei jumped awake when a hand touched his shoulder again. He still felt the geisha's long nails digging into his neck. But it was not Tomomi—only Kazuo looking for help gathering wood to start the cooking fire for breakfast.

As the actors started out on the road again, Seikei's legs felt as if they were made of stone. Tomomi, however, seemed full of life and energy. He did cartwheels along the road, causing a group of travelers to laugh and applaud.

Kazuo dropped back alongside Seikei and asked, "What were the two of you doing last night? You didn't come back from the theater until very late."

Seikei shook his head. "We were rehearsing," he replied.

"Then it's true? That you're getting a role in the play Tomomi is writing?"

Seikei heard the disappointment in Kazuo's voice, and said, "It's only one line."

"But still . . ." Kazuo said, "it will be a very important performance. Tomomi has been telling some of the others that we will appear before the shogun himself."

Seikei stared at him. "That's impossible. Everybody knows samurai are forbidden to attend the kabuki."

Kazuo shrugged. "Samurai often come to our plays. They just disguise themselves as ordinary people."

True enough, Seikei thought, for the judge had brought him to see *The Forty-Seven Ronin*. "But not the shogun," said Seikei.

"People say that the shogun is fond of entertainment," said Kazuo. "He who makes the laws may disobey them, don't you think? Who would punish him? Anyway, it will be interesting to see Edo. I've never been there before."

Seikei was about to reply that he hadn't either, when a sudden blow from behind knocked him sprawling onto the ground. He rolled over and saw Tomomi standing over him.

"Caught you!" laughed Tomomi. "Merchant boy, don't you know that samurai are never off their guard?"

Seikei did know that. The book by Daidoji Yuzan, written for samurai in training, had told him so. "Sleep with one eye open," it had advised. He gritted his teeth and stood up, determined not to let Tomomi catch him again.

But he did. An hour later, when Seikei had been thinking about the sword in Tomomi's trunk, something hard slapped across his cheek.

This time, Seikei realized at once what it was. He whirled and saw Tomomi with a sword. But it was only a play sword, one from the chest of props.

"What do you say?" Tomomi taunted him.

"I swear," replied Seikei, "that I will see you disgraced."

"That's right," Tomomi said with a nod. "Now you have it. You'd like to draw your own sword now and strike me, wouldn't you?"

"Yes," Seikei muttered.

"But you must never do that when you are angry. You will only charge forward blindly and put yourself at the mercy of a swordsman whose mind is calm. Catch your enemy when he does not expect you."

Seikei walked on and after a time became aware that his fatigue had left him. Now that he was truly on guard, and angry, he realized that his senses were sharper. He kept Tomomi always in view and whenever the actor fell back, Seikei slowed his own pace as well. He discovered that he could keep the actor in the corner of his eye.

At the same time, Seikei was searching the crowd on the road for another figure. Judge Ooka had said that Bunzo would follow him, and Seikei looked for the komuso with the basket over his head. He felt that it was important for the judge to know about the real sword in Tomomi's trunk. The threat of its sharp blade hovered over his thoughts. He rubbed his cheek, still smarting from the blow Tomomi had given it, and thought about the scar on Tomomi's own face.

Today when they stopped for lunch, the actors did not have to perform for their meal. They had collected plenty of money from the audience for *The Double Suicide*. Even so, Tomomi approached Seikei with the play sword in his hands. "Like to practice your skills?" the actor asked.

Seikei dreaded what would happen if he accepted. No doubt Tomomi would humiliate him once more, and the others would have a laugh at his expense. He looked around, hoping that Bunzo would suddenly appear to save him. Then Seikei reproached himself. Tomomi had presented a challenge, and he must accept.

Seikei put his bowl of noodles aside and drew his sword, keeping his eyes steadily on Tomomi. "That's right," Tomomi said with a grin. "Two hands, now, remember. Slowly wave it back and forth to keep me at bay. Don't think of it as a wooden sword. It's steel, sharpened to an edge that a fly could not walk on without cutting its feet."

Seikei nodded, knowing that whatever happened

he would learn something, for Tomomi was a master swordsman. Playfully, Tomomi jabbed his own sword forward, and Seikei sidestepped easily.

"Good, good," said Tomomi, "and now . . . prepare to duck!" He sliced his sword through the air toward Seikei's head, and Seikei crouched down so that it would miss. But as he rose, the sword came back again swiftly and this time Seikei narrowly avoided it.

Tomomi gradually increased the speed of his swings and thrusts, and beads of sweat broke out on Seikei's face. Yet, to his surprise, he felt a thrill at the sense of danger. His body responded almost before he asked it to, ducking, jumping, and sliding to the side to avoid Tomomi's blade. Seikei moved in ways that he had not known he was capable of, and he saw Tomomi smile slightly as he too recognized what was happening.

Seikei knew that he was not really winning—Tomomi was not using all his skill. But then he realized how Tomomi intended to end the fight. Just for an instant, Tomomi's eyes gave his intention away. He could not keep from flicking a glance at Seikei's right cheek—the cheek that on Tomomi's own face bore a scar. At once, Seikei understood that was where his opponent would strike, and when Tomomi feinted to the left, Seikei forced himself not to turn with him. In a flash, Tomomi whirled around in a circle, whipping his blade at Seikei from the right. But Seikei had prepared for this. He lashed out with his wooden sword, feeling it knock against Tomomi's hands.

Tomomi's sword fell to the ground.

The other actors roared with amazement, and then delight. "He caught you," they taunted. "The pupil has beaten the master."

For a moment, Tomomi's face darkened, and Seikei felt even greater fear than before. "He let me win," Seikei stammered, but then Tomomi laughed loudly and dropped to his knees. The actor bowed his head to expose his neck. "Finish me off," he said. "Preserve my honor and kill me."

Seikei stepped back, but the other actors pushed him forward. "Go ahead, go ahead," they shouted. "It's *bushido*, the way of the warrior. You must take his head."

Seikei knew that. It was the only honorable action, for a defeated samurai is already dead. He tapped his sword on the back of Tomomi's neck.

"Hai, give him a real knock," urged one of the other actors. He reached for Seikei's sword to do it himself, but suddenly Tomomi was on his feet and caught the man's arm. "This boy has earned the right to kill me, not you," he said. His voice was full of menace, and the other actor retreated, muttering, "Anyway, he beat you."

"Tomomi wasn't using all his skill," Seikei protested again. But Tomomi turned and looked at him with his penetrating eyes. "You won fairly," he said. "I underestimated you. You learn quickly. But, remember, the play will end differently. Then, you must be an actor, not a samurai."

Seikei nodded, glad that Tomomi's anger had cooled so easily.

As they moved out on the road again, Kazuo fell in step beside Seikei. "That was strange," he said. "You know, Tomomi never lets anybody win when he practices. He's too proud. I don't understand it."

Seikei shook his head. He found no joy in the victory. Now that the battle was over, his legs were weak and shaking. He realized that he was leaving himself open to another of Tomomi's surprise attacks, but he could not recover the feeling of sharp awareness he had earlier.

But Tomomi made no more attempts to catch Seikei off guard that day. When the troupe reached the Rokugo River, they paid one of the boatmen there to pole them across. Though this was one of the busiest parts of the great Tokaido Road, a bridge had never been built across the river. According to legend, one of the boatmen's ancestors had rescued Ieyasu, the first Tokugawa shogun, when his enemies were chasing him. In gratitude, Ieyasu had guaranteed that the boatman's descendants would always have the right to ferry travelers across the river.

After the actors crossed, they walked the last stretch of the Tokaido Road. The sun was just setting when they caught sight of the brightly painted roofs of Shinagawa, the pleasure-quarters on the outskirts of the shogun's capital.

A high black gate stood over the road. The shogun's

soldiers were stationed there, questioning travelers, and the actors had to wait. On the left side of the road was a roofed structure that looked like a shrine. Inside, open to view, were many boards with writing on them. These were the edicts of the shogun—warnings and commands to those who were about to enter the city.

Seikei hardly glanced at them, for his eyes froze on a more frightening sight on the other side of the road. Resting on top of a wooden platform were three heads—from executed prisoners who had violated the peace of the shogun's realm. Two of the heads were dry and withered. But the third was fresh, and blood still oozed from it, running down the wood in long streams.

This was a reminder of the shogun's wrath toward those who disobeyed his commands. Seikei knew without reading the boards across the road that one of them prescribed the death penalty for Kirishitans and those who sheltered them. His neck tingled as they approached the checkpoint, for he worried about the gleaming sword in Tomomi's trunk and its scabbard covered with silver crosses.

But when the soldiers questioned them, Tomomi stepped forward and declared that they were traveling kabuki actors, coming to give a performance. Kazuo opened one of the trunks to show their costumes, and the soldiers waved them through.

They had come to the end of the road. They were in Edo, the shogun's city.

~19~

The Shogun's City

They found lodging at an inn in the pleasure quarters. It was noisy, for this was the first night of the midsummer *bon* festival. At this time, the spirits of the dead returned to earth. Throughout the country people discarded their everyday cares to welcome their ancestors.

Seikei thought of what would be happening in his own house in Osaka. Mother would be opening a cask of rice wine to fill the special cups that were used only on this occasion. It was the only time of year when Seikei had ever seen his father drink too much, for he downed cup after cup thanking the spirits of his own father and grandfather for the prosperity of the family business. Even the children were allowed a small measure of sake on this occasion, but mother made sure that they drank only one cup.

The memory made Seikei ache with yearning for home. Somewhere in this great city, his father must also be staying. If only Father knew how Seikei had spent the last few days, what would he think? Seikei shook his head. Perhaps Judge Ooka had reassured Father that Seikei was safe, but it was impossible to predict what the judge might do. On the road Seikei had kept looking for a sign of Bunzo in his disguise as a komuso, but never spied him.

After they ate, Kazuo suggested to Seikei they go outside to watch the festivities. Seikei hesitated. "I think I must rehearse some more with Tomomi," he said.

"Oh, he won't do any work tonight," Kazuo replied. "He's gone off to one of the pleasure-houses already."

Seikei looked around. It was true. Tomomi had slipped away from the other members of the troupe, who were busy draining the bottles of sake provided by the innkeeper. Seikei accused himself of being careless. The judge had told him to follow Tomomi, and now the actor had disappeared.

There was nothing to do but follow Kazuo into the street. It was crowded with revelers celebrating the bon festival. A line of men and women, accompanied by musicians playing drums and samisens, danced through the street as onlookers clapped and sang. Many of the people, Seikei noticed, had been drinking too much sake. Some called out the names of relatives, begging favors from the spirits who had returned from the land of the dead.

Suddenly, a flash of blue silk caught Seikei's eye. One of the dancers moving past the inn was wearing a familiar kimono. Seikei took a step forward, craning his neck to see above the crowd. The flash of blue reappeared—just the sleeve of a kimono, but it drew him forward and then he was running to keep up with it.

It looked very much like the kimono that Tomomi had worn in the play the night before. Seikei could not be certain, but if it was, he had to follow.

The procession of dancers moved down the narrow, twisting street and Seikei, trying to keep up, continually bumped into the people watching from the side. A fat man, laughing, gave him a rough shove, sending Seikei tumbling to the ground.

Jumping up, he touched the hilt of his wooden sword. But he remembered Tomomi's advice not to fight when he was angry. Controlling himself, he ignored the laughing man and rushed after the procession. Now the blue-silk kimono was nowhere in sight. As the dancers reached a teahouse, young women came out to offer cups of sake, and Seikei watched closely as the dancers came forward to accept them.

The hair on the back of his neck tingled as he saw the figure in the blue kimono step forward. Seikei recognized the pins in the dancer's hair, for he had seen them twice before.

Taking the cup, the blue-clad figure turned to face the crowd. Her smiling face was painted white, with vivid red lips and black eyebrows high on the forehead. Only Seikei knew it was not a woman. The figure raised the cup of sake and then poured it on the steps of the teahouse. This gesture brought murmurs of approval from the crowd, for it was meant as an offering to the spirits of the dead.

Tomomi—for it was indeed he, though again assuming not only the clothes but the mannerisms of a woman—then bowed delicately to the teahouse woman, holding out the cup, which she promptly refilled. Tomomi once more turned, confident that all eyes were on him now, and raised the cup to his lips, drinking the liquid down.

The owner of the teahouse could not have wished for a better advertisement. The revelers surged forward to accept their own cups of sake from the women distributing them. Seikei remained where he was, keeping his eyes on the figure in blue. The actor had skillfully caused a scene of confusion in order to make it difficult for anyone to follow him.

Sure enough, as the crowd filled the entrance to the teahouse, Seikei saw Tomomi slip off the steps. In a flash, he disappeared around the corner of the building.

Seikei realized with alarm that he could not push his way through the crowd in time to catch up with Tomomi. He glanced around, and saw another alley on this side of the building. With luck, it might lead to Tomomi.

Seikei ran through the alley, seeing nothing but darkness ahead of him. At the end, his sandals splashed through a stream of foul-smelling water. On either side of him, Seikei could see only a few dim lanterns hung at the back entrances of the row of houses. Which way had Tomomi gone?

Seikei strained to listen. The only sound came from revelers singing inside the houses. Then, at the far end of the deserted little street, he thought he saw another flash of the blue kimono, passing under a lantern.

He ran in that direction, trying not to let his sandals slap against the pebbles on the ground. The street came out into a larger road. It too seemed deserted, but up ahead was a cluster of lanterns that marked a guardhouse. Tomomi must have passed by it already, for he was nowhere to be seen.

As Seikei rushed up to the guardhouse an elderly man tottered out. "What business do you have in this part of the city?" he asked.

Swallowing hard, Seikei replied, "I am in the service of the samurai Judge Ooka, one of the shogun's officials."

The guard's eyebrows went up. "Ooka, you say?" he said. "I thought he was now the magistrate in Kameyama."

"He is pursuing a criminal who has fled to Edo," said Seikei in what he hoped was a confident voice. "The criminal may have come through here just a moment ago."

The old man shook his head. "No one has passed by except a woman from the pleasure quarters, on her way to a daimyo's house." With a wink, he added, "Such great men do not lower themselves by going to that part of the city."

"Was she wearing a blue kimono?" Seikei asked.

"That she was. A beautiful piece of silk. Must have been a gift from her patron. But she'll prosper only while her looks endure. After that . . . " He shrugged.

Seikei tried to conceal his impatience. "What was the name of the daimyo she was going to visit?"

"Lord Hakuseki."

Seikei blinked. Why would Tomomi be going to the house of the man whose jewel he had stolen? To rob him again?

"I must go there," Seikei said. "It is urgent. Can you tell me the way?"

"Just follow this street," the guard said. "It's a grand house, one of the largest in Edo, excepting the shogun's castle, of course. Do you know the Hakuseki crest?"

"Yes. A red fish with a box around it."

"Go ahead then. You'll see it on the gate. But you won't get past his guards with the story you've told me."

Seikei could not keep himself from asking, "Then why are you letting me pass?"

The guard's wrinkled face broke into a smile. "Because you mentioned the name of Ooka. He saved me

161

from disgrace once. When you see him, tell him that Itagawa Yokio has not forgotten him." He bowed, an action that Seikei knew was meant for the man he served.

Seikei returned the bow and hurried on down the street. The moon had risen, giving enough light for him to find his way. But high stone walls shielded the houses on either side, and the wooden gates were tightly shut. If there were any celebrations of the bon festival in this part of the city, they were private ones.

Seikei felt the presence of the spirits of the dead all around him. Some, it was said, came back to avenge wrongs that had been committed against them in life. Seikei wished he were home in Osaka now, where the only spirits were the benign ones of his ancestors, welcomed back to the home they had helped to build.

I need fear no spirit, Seikei reminded himself. Then a breeze from nowhere ruffled his hair, eerily, like someone touching him.

For some reason, Seikei remembered the inn-keeper back in Kameyama, where all this had begun. He had given a room to Seikei and his father. That had been the man's misfortune, because it was Seikei's sleeplessness that helped the judge to discover the tunnel under the inn. That in turn had caused the innkeeper to kill himself rather than confess. Seikei closed his eyes, but that did not blot out the image of the man's face. I am sorry, he thought. I did not know what would happen to you.

Suddenly afraid, he hurried on, though he knew it was impossible to move faster than a spirit. He heard hoofbeats on the road in front of him and moved to the side just in time, for a mounted samurai galloped by in a hurry. Seikei knew that the man would have ridden over him without a backward glance.

Seikei straightened his back. I too have a duty to perform, he thought. Still, he shivered as the hoofbeats died away, for the street seemed more silent than before. All the house-fronts had their shutters slid tightly closed, and the gates were tied shut with ropes on which bells hung to waken the occupants if anyone tried to loosen them. There were no lights to be seen, for people feared starting fires that could spread rapidly through houses made of thin pine and paper walls.

Seikei stopped suddenly. Somewhere behind him he had heard a footstep. Or had he? There was no sound now, except the whisper of leaves brushing against each other. Or perhaps the innkeeper's spirit, still pursuing him.

There was nothing to do but go on. The road wound through the city, and smaller streets led off of it. The guard had not mentioned those, and after a while Seikei began to wonder if he had lost his way.

Then the wind rose and he heard a sound like the flapping of the wings of a great bird. Instinctively, Seikei covered his head with his hands. After a moment he peered cautiously into the sky. At the top of a hill, the moon shone on a fluttering banner with a red fish with a box around it—Lord Hakuseki's crest.

As Seikei cautiously approached, he was awed by the size of the house. Indeed, it was not a single house, but a *yashiki,* a large group of buildings where the daimyo's samurai and family lived. A high wall with glistening tiles surrounded the yashiki. Seikei could dimly make out the figures of guards on watch at the top. He ducked into the shadows at the base of the wall.

It was clear that nothing Seikei could say would gain him admission to the house in the middle of the night. But Tomomi must have entered, perhaps because he was dressed as a geisha. If Tomomi had truly made up his mind to get inside, nothing would stop him.

But what was Tomomi's purpose in coming here at all? If his disguise were discovered, he would be imprisoned, or more likely executed on the spot.

Judge Ooka had told Seikei to follow Tomomi because there might be another criminal in the case. Seikei had obeyed, only to find that Tomomi's path led back to the man from whom he had stolen the jewel. Evidently, Tomomi had not finished whatever his mission was.

No, the actor was inside Lord Hakuseki's yashiki, for certain. So it was Seikei's duty to wait here until he came out—alive or dead.

-20-

A Promise to the Spirits

Waiting was difficult when you did not know how long it would take. Seikei knew by heart the stories of many brave samurai, but all of them had distinguished themselves through their honor and courage. It took no courage to wait, only patience. Seikei forced himself to think of Oishi, the leader of the Forty-Seven Ronin. Oishi had waited for more than a year before taking revenge for his lord's death, all the while enduring the insults of those who thought he had abandoned the code of the samurai. Yet Oishi never wavered, never . . .

Seikei suddenly snapped awake. He had not even realized that he had been sleeping, but he saw that the night was even darker now. The moon had slipped behind a cloud. Something had awakened him, though. He remembered it intruding on his dream.

What was it? A footstep? The sound of rustling silk? He held his breath, straining to hear the sound again. Nothing.

But someone had passed by him as he dozed. He was sure of it. It must have been Tomomi. Who else could have emerged from Lord Hakuseki's yashiki?

Seikei rose and ran down the street the way he had come, trying to keep his sandals from slapping against the stones. At the first cross street, he peered in both directions, trying to pierce the inky black shadows. Which way? Which way? There! He had heard the sound again. He rushed on blindly through the darkness in pursuit of it.

All at once, he was grabbed from behind. He felt his face enveloped in silk. Seikei opened his mouth to cry out, but could not. A sweet-smelling perfume filled his nostrils, and his muscles grew weak. He clawed at the silk, desperately trying to pull it away from his face. But the arm beneath the silk was too strong.

Then he remembered his sword. With the last of his strength, Seikei drew it from his obi and flailed upward, feeling it strike something hard. He heard a gasp, and felt the attacker's hold loosen.

Seikei wrenched free, turning to face his assailant. Both hands on the hilt of the sword, legs apart in the fighting stance, he prepared for another attack.

A high-pitched giggle echoed through the street. "You again," came a woman's voice, which Seikei recognized. "I taught you too well, didn't I?"

"Why are you talking like that?" said Seikei. "I know who you are."

"Really? Then you know me better than I do," replied the silky voice. "Especially on this night, when the spirits return." Tomomi leaned close; his white-painted face shone like the moon itself. "Have you seen them?" he whispered.

The question sent a shiver through Seikei's body.

Tomomi noticed. Nothing ever escaped his piercing eyes. "There's no reason to fear them," he said. "They return to see what we have done to honor them. Through us, they can enter the land of the living once more. It is a time to be happy."

He put his hand on Seikei's shoulder. "Put your sword away," he said, in a voice more like a man's now. "There is no need for it. I heard you following—you should learn more about the art of silence, by the way—and I thought you were one of Lord Hakuseki's men."

"But you came from there," Seikei blurted out.

"So you *did* follow me," Tomomi said. "Well, no matter. You remember the line I taught you?"

"I swear that I will see you disgraced," Seikei replied dutifully.

"You hear?" Tomomi cried joyfully, whirling around and raising his voice into the darkness around them. "Mother? Father? Tomorrow I will keep my promise to you."

Seikei looked nervously around, feeling the pres-

167

ence of the spirits he could not see. Tomomi started down the street. "Come then," he said. "Let us return to the others and begin work on the play. We have only a day to rehearse. And the performance must be perfect, for the shogun himself will be present."

Seikei rushed to keep up with him. "The shogun? How can that be?"

"Through the generosity—and vanity—of Lord Hakuseki," Tomomi explained. "The shogun, you see, has a secret fondness for the kabuki plays, but of course he cannot go to a public theater, even in disguise as so many samurai do. So Lord Hakuseki has employed our troupe to give a special performance in his yashiki. The lord wishes to impress the shogun. Now that he cannot make him a present of that marvelous rare jewel, which has mysteriously disappeared, he will surprise him with a kabuki performance. And indeed it will be an unforgettable evening."

The sound of Tomomi's laughter rose into the sky like a flock of geese. And it was true—Seikei felt the spirits respond. Perhaps it was only Tomomi's voice echoing down the deserted streets, but it sounded to Seikei like the dead speaking. What were they saying? He strained to hear, but he could not make out the words.

21

The Rehearsal

Seikei and Tomomi made their way back to the inn where the rest of the troupe was staying. Seikei lay down on a mat and immediately fell asleep. But his rest was brief, for as soon as the sun was up, Tomomi—now in his own clothing—awakened everyone. It was time to rehearse, he announced. Tonight they would perform for the shogun.

The play he had written was an elaborate one. Kazuo emptied the trunks, looking for costumes and props. "Find the rosaries and crucifixes," Tomomi commanded. Everyone knew that meant there were going to be Kirishitans in the play.

The Kirishitan religion had arrived in Japan almost two hundred years before, brought by foreign devils from a distant country beyond China. A powerful daimyo named Oda Nobunaga allowed Kirishitan priests to preach their religion within his domains. Some Japanese became Kirishitans, and for a time it was popular to wear Kirishitan symbols as jewelry.

After Nobunaga's death, his ally Ieyasu Tokugawa was named shogun, or military commander of Japan. His descendants had held the post ever since. Because the Tokugawas feared that the Kirishitans were plotting a rebellion, they banned the religion and executed any Kirishitans who clung to their faith.

Even so, it was rumored that some Japanese continued to practice the religion, though they risked the death penalty for doing so. Seikei, growing up in Osaka, had sometimes heard that people kept shrines to Kirishitan saints hidden inside their houses. Seikei's father had always told him to pay no attention to these stories.

Tomomi's play began in the household of a daimyo whose family had, in fact, secretly kept the Kirishitan religion during all the years when it had been banned. The hair on the back of Seikei's neck tingled when he heard the family name: Takezaki. The play would be the story of Tomomi's own family.

And now Tomomi pointed to him, saying, "You will play the eldest son." The actor locked his eyes on Seikei's, and added, "Your name is Genji."

Seikei nodded, knowing that it was a kind of honor: he was to be Tomomi's younger self.

Kazuo could not keep from showing his disappointment. "How can you let him play a role? He is no actor."

"A better one than you suspect," Tomomi shot back.

"You promised that *I* could go on stage someday," Kazuo persisted.

Tomomi shrugged. "Very well. We'll let you appear as a servant, then. But you'll die horribly when the play is only half over."

Kazuo looked pleased. "Very horribly?" he asked.

"As dreadful a death as we can imagine for you," Tomomi muttered.

The excitement shone on Kazuo's face.

The other actors expected Tomomi himself to take the role of Lord Takezaki, the head of the family, but he assigned it to another actor. "I will play his wife," Tomomi announced. "Faithful to her husband, devoted to her son, beautiful, wise, and courageous—as a true samurai woman should be, for her family too was a noble one."

"In addition to these qualities, does she have a name?" someone asked sarcastically.

Tomomi gave the man a look that made Seikei shiver. "Nanaho, daughter of a branch of the Fujiwaras, the most noble family in Japan," he replied coldly.

Seikei wished that Tomomi was playing another role, for he had not forgotten how strange the actor became when he donned women's clothes. But the others approved, for they knew that Tomomi's appearance on stage as a female was popular with audiences.

It seemed to Seikei that no one else suspected that there was a deeper meaning to the play. Even Kazuo, who had heard Tomomi proclaim himself as Genji, son of Takezaki Kita, was too caught up in the excitement of his first stage appearance to let that bother him.

The first scenes of the play were happy ones, showing a family lovingly devoted to each other. For the audience, the interest would be the strange Kirishitan rituals that the Takezakis practiced in secret rooms known only to their servants—who were Kirishitans as well. Portraying Kirishitans on stage was acceptable, as long as they eventually came to an unhappy end.

And as the play developed, that fate soon seemed inevitable. For a neighboring daimyo learned the secret of the Takezakis. The role was assigned to Yukio, the actor who had played the father of the tragic lover in the troupe's previous play. This time, he was outfitted in a grand and spectacular costume. His clothing was padded and stiffened at the shoulders to make him seem a giant of a man. His helmet was crowned with a golden sunburst that added a full two feet to his height. But the effect was spoiled because Yukio was barely able to walk in the costume. As he waddled across the floor, the helmet slipped over his eyes and the elaborate garments constantly threatened to trip him up.

"I need someone to help me walk," Yukio complained to Tomomi.

"No, you're perfect," Tomomi replied. "Lord Shakuheki must be an immense figure, showing his ambition to be great."

Lord Shakuheki? When Seikei heard the name, he knew who the enemy of the Takezaki family really was. Tomomi had barely attempted to disguise it. But what could the actor be thinking of? To put on this play, to mock Lord Hakuseki in this manner—in his own house! It was madness.

Yet Seikei could do nothing about it. The other members of the troupe trusted Tomomi's promise that they would perform before the shogun himself. It was a great opportunity for them. During breaks in the rehearsal, it was all anyone talked about. Perhaps, some said, the shogun would reward them if the performance pleased him.

The plot continued to unfold. Lord Shakuheki had once wished to marry Nanaho, but she persuaded her parents to accept the offer of another man—Takezaki Kita. Lord Shakuheki's pride was wounded, but he concealed his bitterness, pretending to be a friend, until he discovered that Takezaki was a Kirishitan and his wife had adopted the religion.

Lord Shakuheki hatched his plans to destroy the Takezaki family. He sent a messenger to the shogun, asking permission to search for Kirishitans and execute them. Then he visited Nanaho to warn her. "My samurai are as many as the grains of sand on the beach," he bragged. "Your husband, who has violated the decree of the shogun, cannot resist me. I will have his head. But I offer you a chance to save your life. If you renounce your religion, I will spare you and your son."

Tomomi, in his role as Nanaho, faced the lord with contempt. Though he wore no makeup, Tomomi easily became a woman again. "You are a man without honor," she replied. "You have treacherously used our friendship to betray my trust in you. Who could accept such an offer and live?" With that, she turned and left.

Nanaho told her husband of the danger, and the Takezakis prepared to fight. Calling their servants and samurai together, they prayed to the Kirishitan god. Kazuo, as one of the servants, raised his voice loudly in the words that Tomomi had written. And then, Tomomi brought an object from his kimono, holding it high before the assembled company.

Seikei saw with shock that it was a large golden crucifix—with a red jewel at the top of the cross! He could hardly believe it. He had seen Judge Ooka smash one such ruby at the inn, and witnessed Tomomi leave another at the shrine of Amaterasu. Yet now there was a third. Could it be the real one?

Tomomi, as Nanaho, prayed to the strange god who

hung on the cross. "All who follow the Lord Kirist," she said, "know that a paradise awaits those who die in his name. And as samurai, we know that honor demands it."

The next scene was the battle in which Lord Shakuheki's men attacked the Takezaki castle. It was bloody enough to please any audience, for the loyal Takezaki retainers fought furiously. Yet one by one, they died before the swords of the invaders. Kazuo, playing the faithful servant, had his head cut off (a false one, tossed onto the stage as Kazuo hid his real head under his costume). But Kazuo continued his loud cries of agony until he was sharply informed that without a head, he must silently accept his death.

Takezaki Kita, Genji's father, was among the last to die. As he fell, his wife rushed forward to grasp his sword. She fought off Lord Shakuheki's men and escaped, taking her son with her. At the edge of the stage, she handed him the sword in its scabbard. "Take this," she said, "and flee. Lord Shakuseki will not pursue you, for my death is all that he desires."

Seikei, playing the role of Genji, accepted the sword. He saw that it was the one he had found in Tomomi's trunk, and now understood its secret.

With that, Nanaho stabbed herself, choosing the honorable death of seppuku.

The waddling figure of Lord Shakuheki now appeared. He discovered Nanaho's body and took the jeweled cross from her kimono, raising it high in triumph. But Genji rushed forward to confront him.

The actor playing Lord Shakuheki drew his own sword and slashed him across the face. As Tomomi directed, the blow struck Genji across the right cheek. Seikei pressed his hand to his cheek, smearing a concealed oilskin packet of red paint across his face.

And now . . . the line he had rehearsed so many times: "I swear that I will see you disgraced," shouted Seikei, and leaped through a window, escaping the fate of the others.

The cast agreed that the play was a thrilling one, though some pointed out to Tomomi that the last line was puzzling. It left the audience wanting another scene.

"There is one more scene," said Tomomi, "but Yukio and I will rehearse it together."

"Will you appear in it?"

"Yes. He and I are the only characters."

"Then Nanaho will return to Lord Shakuheki as a ghost? What does she say?"

But Tomomi only shook his head mysteriously. "It will be a surprise," he said. "You will learn it tonight, when we perform the play for the shogun."

Of course, everyone wanted to know the secret now, but Tomomi refused to let the others watch. "Get something to eat," he said. "Then pack the costumes and props. We will leave for the performance at sundown."

Seikei followed the others out of the room. Though he too was curious about the last scene, his head was buzzing with everything he had learned. If only there were some way to find Judge Ooka! Tomomi's motive for stealing the jewel was now clear. And the jewel itself might not be resting at the shrine of Amaterasu— Tomomi might have put a false one there, knowing that Seikei would tell the judge.

Suddenly a voice interrupted Seikei's thoughts. "What did you think of it?"

It was Kazuo, grinning broadly.

"The play?" replied Seikei. "The play is a crazy—"

"No, I mean my performance," said Kazuo. "Do you think the shogun will like it?"

Seikei shook his head ruefully. "Kazuo," he said, "don't you remember the night when Tomomi said that *he* was Genji, the son of Takezaki Kita?"

"The night he took your sword away? That didn't mean anything." Kazuo chuckled. "Tomomi was just writing the play in his head. He always pretends he's one of the characters. He never stops acting, even when he's off stage. It's one of the things that makes the teahouse girls fall in love with him."

"But the play is true," Seikei insisted. "And tonight we're going to perform it for Lord Hakuseki. He's the real Lord Shakuheki. It's obvious. Don't you see? This is part of Tomomi's revenge."

"Oh, no. You're wrong," said Kazuo confidently. "Nobody would be that foolish. If that were true, the lord would probably kill us all."

Seikei nodded grimly. That was exactly what would

happen. His only hope was that Judge Ooka had guessed correctly where the path would lead. He sighed. Not even the judge could know that. But Seikei was pledged to follow it to the very end.

22

The Performance

Seikei had not been able to eat. He was too nervous about what might happen at the performance of the play. All afternoon, he had drunk cups of tea, trying to calm his stomach. The tea had only caused him to become more restless. His mind returned over and over to the story of Tomomi, the wandering actor, the samurai, the thief.

Each time Seikei had thought he had solved the puzzle, Tomomi did something that caused a new mystery. When Seikei discovered that Tomomi had taken the jewel, Tomomi surprised him by leaving it at the shrine of Amaterasu. Then Seikei found that Tomomi was indeed the samurai he claimed to be. He had a samurai's sword, and knew the skills it took to use it. But then why did he follow the life of a kabuki actor?

Seikei kept thinking nervously about the real sword

that he had discovered in Tomomi's trunk. For a brief moment, Seikei had held it on stage during the rehearsal, but his role had not required him to draw it from the scabbard. It remained hidden, like the secrets that Tomomi had yet to reveal.

At sunset, the troupe gathered their trunks and set out for Lord Hakuseki's yashiki. In the streets, the celebration of the bon festival was still going on, but Seikei paid no attention to the merrymaking. He said a silent prayer to his own ancestors, but sensed that they were far away in Osaka and could not find him here.

At the checkpoint to the inner city, Tomomi showed a paper and the guard waved them through. The troupe made their way through the winding streets, finally arriving at Lord Hakuseki's yashiki, where the banner with his mon flew over the gate. But the guards there would not let them through, even after Tomomi showed his paper.

Seikei felt a sudden surge of hope. Perhaps they would be unable to enter, and have to return to the inn. But no. It was only that lowly kabuki actors could not pass through the main gate, which was reserved for nobles and samurai. Instead, they had to proceed around the wall to a lesser gate meant for tradespeople and merchants.

At the side gate, a servant was waiting, and let them inside. As Seikei filed through with the others, he realized that this was a perfect way to smuggle a sword inside the yashiki. No one bothered to look inside the trunks the troupe carried. No one thought them worthy of a second glance.

Inside they passed through a splendid garden. Even in the twilight, Seikei could see that it was planted with gorgeous flowers and trees that were pruned neatly into shapes that dazzled the eye. It was a breathtaking sight, one that must have required dozens of gardeners to maintain. But after a second, Seikei thought of the simple rock garden at Judge Ooka's house. The judge's garden invited the viewer to look within himself. The one in Lord Hakuseki's yashiki forced people to contemplate the greatness of the man who owned it. And of course, a truly great man would never do that.

The servant led the troupe into a great hall. "Here is where the lord entertains his guests," said the servant. "Prepare swiftly, for they arrive soon."

As Seikei looked around, he saw that there was no place for an audience to watch the play. "Where will the daimyo's guests sit?" he asked.

Tomomi pointed to tall bamboo screens that sat around the walls of the hall. "Behind those," he said. "The daimyo and his guests are too high in rank to let actors look upon them. It would wound the shogun's dignity to reveal that he was watching our performance."

"But how can they see us through the screens?"

"Go and look."

Seikei slipped behind one of the tall screens. Though it was dark here, he could feel comfortable cushions resting on the floor. When he turned, he could see the actors lighting lanterns on the stage. The slits between the strips of bamboo in the screen were wide enough to see through.

He was disappointed. He was curious to see what the shogun looked like, but even more he wanted to know if Judge Ooka had followed the correct path and come to attend the performance. It was a slim hope, but his only one.

The traveling troupe was accustomed to set up their performances in the courtyards of shrines, in Buddhist monastery halls, even in an empty field if that was the only place for an audience to gather. A kabuki performance depends on the ability of the actors to create a scene in the imagination of the audience, so there is little scenery. A hiding place, a rock from which lovers can leap, or a wall with a doorway or window—like the one Seikei would use to escape—are all that is necessary. Colored lanterns, the musicians, and the actors' skill do the rest. It did not take long to prepare for the performance.

Still, Seikei sensed some nervousness among the actors as they dressed for their roles. This would be the most important performance of their lives.

Kazuo helped him put on makeup and found a kimono that indicated Seikei's status as the son of a daimyo. As usual, Tomomi had gone behind his own screen to conceal his preparations. Nobody would see him until it was time for him to go on stage. "It's a great night for us," Kazuo whispered. "Everybody is hoping we'll get a big present from the daimyo if the shogun is pleased."

Seikei didn't have the heart to warn Kazuo that he would consider them lucky to escape with their lives. "How will we be able to tell what they think of the performance?" he asked. "We can't even see them."

"We did this kind of thing, performing in front of screens, once before at a monastery," Kazuo replied. "Watch the screens. If the people really like what they see, the slits will open wider."

There was no time to ask how that was possible. They had barely finished dressing when the daimyo's servant appeared. "The guests are seating themselves," he said. "Do not make them wait."

The musicians took their places at the side of the stage. Looking at each other, they nodded. Clack! Clack! went the wooden clappers, and the play was on.

Seikei was among those in the first scene. He carried a rosary in a procession that let the audience know that the family were Kirishitans. Tomomi had scheduled dances and songs to enliven this part. One member of the troupe performed magic tricks. The audience accepted all this as part of the Kirishitan religion.

The troupe's magician was particularly good

tonight, emptying his bag of tricks. Seikei was close enough to see that he hid some kind of powder in his hand before thrusting a sword into a lantern. Suddenly flames ran down the blade of the sword, and the actor waved it about the stage. Acrobats responded by turning backflips as if to escape from him.

Seikei had been too nervous to look toward the bamboo screens. But when he heard crackling sounds, he glanced out in the direction of the audience. Some of the onlookers had thrust folding fans between the strips of bamboo. By unfolding the fans, they opened the slits wider. Seikei caught a glimpse of an eye staring at him before he turned back to his stage business.

The music rang out faster, with the dancers following suit, their bright-colored robes streaming behind them. Seikei realized that Kazuo was right: the troupe was displaying all the skills they could summon, and truly the performance was splendid. Then, when the stage was filled with color and movement, a graceful figure appeared, clad in blue silk.

The dancers stopped in position, as if they had suddenly turned to stone. All eyes went to Tomomi, playing his own mother. She broke into a song that gradually rose above the music. Dancing across the stage, she glided past the other actors like a leaf blown by the wind.

Tomomi surpassed the simple illusion that he was a woman: he became a goddess come to earth. Seikei heard the crackling of the screens all around the stage as the audience sought to get a better look. Seikei himself could not take his eyes off Tomomi.

She sang of the two men who loved her. One offered her his purity of heart and devotion to honor. The other offered her wealth and luxury. She made the only choice that a samurai woman could.

Behind him, Seikei heard a muffled cry. Lord Hakuseki had recognized the plot of the play. Seikei stiffened, waiting for a more violent reaction. But nothing happened as Tomomi finished the song, telling of the birth of her son. Now she danced to where Seikei stood. As she placed her arms around him, the stage went dark.

Quickly, the actors rose and reassembled for the next scene, a banquet at which their neighbor Lord Shakuheki was the guest of honor. Yukio, playing the daimyo, seemed more ridiculous than ever in contrast to the grace and beauty of Tomomi's performance. Seikei heard chuckles behind the screens that concealed the audience.

But behind one screen there was an ominous silence.

Seikei, seated at the edge of the stage for the banquet, cautiously looked at the silent screen. There was no fan holding open the slits; a large hand, with shining gold rings on two fingers, pressed down on the bamboo strips. Seikei had seen those rings before— they belonged to Lord Hakuseki.

As the play continued, it was clear that most of the audience were enjoying themselves. Like the actors, they assumed that the play was a tragedy in which the Takezaki family had doomed themselves by following the banned Kirishitan religion. The music and dances that accompanied the action were sometimes so entertaining that some behind the bamboo screens applauded.

The troupe played the battle scene for all the thrills they could draw from it. By now, the slits in the bamboo screens were open all around the hall, and Seikei heard the onlookers exclaim with pleasure at each bloody death. Kazuo must have been proud at the gasps that greeted his severed head bouncing across the stage.

When Tomomi had held up the cross with the red jewel, Seikei tensed himself again, knowing that Lord Hakuseki would recognize it. Hearing the clatter of bamboo strips, Seikei could not help looking in that direction. Lord Hakuseki had withdrawn his hand, letting the screen snap shut.

Of course! Everything was suddenly clear. That must have been Tomomi's plan. Lord Hakuseki could not interrupt the play with the shogun present. He would reveal that he was humiliated by the scenes that were taking place on stage—by a kabuki troupe that he had invited to perform at his own yashiki. He had to control his anger, for a daimyo was forbidden to draw his sword in the presence of the shogun. If Lord

Hakuseki did so, he would face the same penalty as the lord of the Forty-Seven Ronin. He would be forced to kill himself.

So now, as the play drew closer to its climax, Seikei understood how significant were the words that he was to speak at the end of the scene. While the samurai of Lord Shakuseki battered at the door, Tomomi clasped Seikei and led him to the side of the stage.

Looking into the actor's eyes, Seikei felt himself drawn into the past. He became Genji, the real Tomomi. He understood the sorrow and the anger that had made Tomomi pursue Lord Hakuseki for years until this night, when he would avenge his honor.

As his mother gave him his father's sword, Genji felt its strength flow into his arm. It would sustain him, help him bear the pain of her loss, for he knew that now she must commit seppuku.

And as she did, thrusting the sword into her body with a little cry, her eyes bored into those of her son, telling him that he must not, ever, forget his promise.

So when Lord Shakuheki the actor appeared on stage, Seikei needed no coaching to rush toward him with the desire for revenge. It took self-control for Seikei to play the scene as Tomomi had written it. He accepted the slash across his face, pressing his hand there to break the packet of blood.

As he felt it run down his cheek, he realized that the music had stopped and the hall was silent. Everyone was waiting for the words he had to say, and this time they came from the heart of Genji, a heart that Seikei now understood very well.

He heard the words as if someone else was speaking them: "I swear that I will see you disgraced." In a flash, Seikei leaped through the window, and the stage lanterns went out.

All around the hall, behind the bamboo screens, Seikei heard muffled conversations. The sound of puzzlement was in the air. Like the actors in rehearsal, the audience wondered if that was really the end of the play.

But the music resumed, indicating that something more was to come, and the buzz of voices slowly died down. In the darkness, Seikei felt someone come up beside him. "I will need this," he heard Tomomi murmur as the actor took the sword from his hands.

Startled, Seikei turned to ask a question, but Tomomi was already gone. There was nothing for Seikei to do but join the other actors behind the stage, waiting to see what secrets the final scene would reveal.

23

The Play Is Finished

A single lantern, raised high above the stage on a pole, revealed Lord Shakuheki sleeping on a mat. Beside him lay his two swords and a small black casket decorated with red leaves. Seikei saw with alarm that it was a duplicate of the casket from which the real jewel had been stolen.

The musicians played an eerie tune that summoned up images of spirits that walked in the night. Remembering the bon festival, Seikei glanced around the dark hall. He nearly cried out when he saw the ghost approaching.

Strips of white silk fluttered behind the figure. As it moved silently under the lantern, its white face glowed. Two dark eyes, lit with passion, turned toward the screens. This time, Seikei did not mistake the pins in its hair for horns. The ghost of the Tokaido Inn had returned to repeat its crime.

In his mother's voice, Tomomi denounced Lord Shakuheki for his treachery and dishonor, hurling insult after insult down onto the sleeping form.

"Yet in spite of your wealth and power, even though you have prospered from the lands you stole from my family, you still yearn for more. For something still eludes you, doesn't it?" She laughed, mocking him so cruelly that Seikei could not understand how the real Lord Hakuseki could stand it.

"What you desire is respect," the ghost said, nearly spitting out the last word. "The respect that a truly great samurai should have. But at the shogun's court, you are merely tolerated, not given a place of honor. For the shogun, like everyone who comes into your presence, sees you for what you are. A man without honor."

Seikei wanted to get up and cry out for Tomomi to stop. He was going too far.

But the voice went on relentlessly. "So now you are bringing him a gift," she said. "A great treasure that you think will awe him. And like the honorless man you are, you chose a gift that you have stolen."

She bent down and opened the lacquered casket. Removing the jewel, she held it high so that its dark red color shone in the lantern light. "This is your gift," she said. "I now claim it as mine, and I will be the one to give it to the shogun."

A tremendous crash came from the darkness at the side of the hall. Lord Hakuseki could not endure his shame any longer. Seikei saw him burst through the bamboo screen, tearing away the scraps of wood that clung to his clothing. "Thief!" he shouted. "I know who you are. I should have killed you!"

The actor playing Lord Shakuheki opened his eyes, took a terrified look at what was happening, and scrambled off to a safer place. Tomomi remained where he stood at center stage. A broad smile swept across his face. "What is this I see?" he cried. "A ghost? A dream? No, it is the dishonorable wretch himself!"

Behind the other screens, the unseen members of the audience began to cry out. Some thought this was part of the play, but others seemed to realize that something dreadful was happening.

"Is this yours?" Tomomi taunted, holding out the jewel. "Take it from me if you can—thief! For truly I am Genji, the son of Takezaki Kita, from whom you stole this jewel."

Challenged, Lord Hakuseki lost control. He drew his sword and furiously charged toward Tomomi. Screams and shouts echoed through the hall, but Seikei riveted his eyes on the scene under the lantern. Lord Hakuseki slashed Tomomi's white silk kimono to ribbons, but then stood foolishly as the pieces of it fluttered around him. It was empty.

Tomomi had slipped off the robe with one swift motion and escaped into the shadows. As Lord Hakuseki looked around, Tomomi reappeared. Under the kimono, he wore the costume of the samurai Oishi, the leader of the Forty-Seven Ronin. At his side, he wore the traditional two swords, and Seikei recognized one by the silver crosses on its scabbard.

Now, slowly and reverently, Tomomi drew the shining steel blade from its sheath. "It's real!" Seikei heard Kazuo cry out from somewhere in the hall, but everyone else understood that already—even Lord Hakuseki, who took an uncertain step backward.

Tomomi moved toward him, step by step, waving the sword back and forth. It sliced through the air with a noise like a swarm of bees.

"Stop!" someone shouted from behind the screens. "The shogun is present!" But neither Tomomi nor Lord Hakuseki seemed to hear. Their eyes locked, and the daimyo raised his sword. Immediately, Tomomi struck out with his own blade, which moved so swiftly that it was impossible for the eye to follow it. A crimson line appeared on the daimyo's right cheek, and blood began to flow from it.

Lord Hakuseki lunged forward, desperately trying to impale Tomomi on his sword, but the actor danced out of the way. "Remember?" he called, mocking the daimyo. "Do you remember me?" He moved under Lord Hakuseki's clumsy thrusts a second time, and now slashed his other cheek.

More bamboo screens were now crashing down, and people shouted for the guards stationed outside the hall. Seikei paid no attention, for he had lost all fear of the consequences. He watched Tomomi's sword strike again and again.

Lord Hakuseki's clothing was soaked with blood. He could barely hold his sword in front of him. It was clear that his skill was so inferior to Tomomi's that the actor could have killed him, yet he refused to do so.

Seikei understood. To kill him would have saved Lord Hakuseki from disgrace. Death in battle was the most honorable way for a samurai to die. Tomomi intended to dishonor Lord Hakuseki so completely that he could not bear to live.

Five samurai, with the shogun's crest on their headbands, surrounded Tomomi. He gave them a brief glance, and then knelt. Setting his sword down, he untied his kimono and peeled it back from his neck. One of the samurai looked across the room. All the screens had fallen by now, revealing only one person still seated on the cushions. This man calmly nodded and waved his hand in a sign of approval.

The shogun's samurai drew his sword and brought it down through Tomomi's neck with one stroke. The actor's head fell to the floor and a torrent of blood gushed from his body. His hand opened, and as Seikei watched, the precious ruby tumbled into the crimson flood on the floor.

Slowly, Tomomi's head rolled over. Its eyes remained open, and Seikei saw that in death, Tomomi's face wore a triumphant smile.

Someone stepped between Seikei and the gruesome sight. Numbed by what he had witnessed, Seikei dimly recognized the man, but had to struggle to remember who he was.

Judge Ooka reached down to close Tomomi's eyes. He stood up and walked over to Seikei. "Now you have seen a samurai die," the judge said. "Was it the way you imagined it to be?"

-24-

A Tea Ceremony

"Wake up! You're not at home now, merchant's son, where you can spend all day long in idleness!"

The voice was Bunzo's. Seikei's eyes fluttered open. He was glad to be awakened. He had been dreaming of running through the streets of Edo in the darkness, trying to escape from a bloody head floating through the air.

He breathed a sigh of relief when he saw that he was in an ordinary room where the sun shone brightly through a paper window. Daylight meant that he was safe, and that Tomomi's spirit . . .

"Is the bon festival over?" he asked.

"Of course."

"Then the spirits have left?"

"Stop talking about spirits," said Bunzo. "You kept

me awake all night with your dreams. Get up and wash yourself. If you're late, the judge will blame me."

Seikei dimly remembered that Judge Ooka had taken him away from Lord Hakuseki's yashiki and brought him to this house. Seikei hadn't even remembered falling asleep.

"Late for what?"

"*Cha-no-yu,* a tea ceremony. Have you ever been to one?"

Bunzo's sarcastic tone indicated that he thought that was unlikely. So Seikei was pleased to respond, "Yes, I have. My father is a merchant of tea. I had to learn the ceremony so that I could be present when he welcomes business associates."

"Humph!" snorted Bunzo. "A merchant's tea ceremony. Now that would be something to see."

"Is the judge having a tea ceremony?" asked Seikei.

"No, but he'll be there. Hurry up. Time for questions later."

Seikei washed himself, and then dressed in the clean clothing that Bunzo provided. Proudly, Seikei saw that it was the plain jacket and leggings that samurai in the service of great lords usually wore. But when he began to tie his wooden sword around his waist, Bunzo stopped him. "No swords at a tea ceremony," he said.

Seikei was embarrassed. He should have remembered. When samurai and daimyos attended tea ceremonies, they left behind all the things that marked their rank. The ceremony was supposed to be an occasion where all who took part were equal.

Outside, two horses were saddled and waiting, and Seikei recognized the slow old horse that he had first used when accompanying the judge to Ise. "You managed to stay on it before," said Bunzo. "Try to do so now. We will not have far to go."

The streets were filled with people hurrying back and forth. All the shops were open now, and Seikei understood why his father often talked of opening a store in Edo. So many customers, and it was often said that the people of the shogun's capital were spendthrifts, willing to pay far more for goods than those in other cities.

With Bunzo leading the way, they passed through the commercial district into the area where the great daimyos lived. Seikei saw some yashiki that were even larger than Lord Hakuseki's. The tragic outcome of Tomomi's play crept into his mind, and Seikei suddenly wondered what happened to the rest of the actors. "Were you at Lord Hakuseki's yashiki last night?" he asked Bunzo.

The samurai shook his head. "You'll hear about that from the judge, if he wishes to tell you," he said.

They turned a corner and Seikei saw an immense wall that stretched far down the street. He caught his breath. This was a yashiki that was so huge that it dwarfed any other in the city. In fact, it must be . . .

"Is this the shogun's palace?" he asked.

Bunzo nodded. "That's where you're going."

Seikei felt his stomach jump. "Aren't you coming with me?"

Bunzo gave him a little smile, the first time he had ever shown any sympathy for Seikei. "It's a great honor. I was there once, but my orders are to turn you over to the guards."

When they reached the entrance, Bunzo dismounted and Seikei followed. Bunzo spoke a few words to the samurai at the entrance, and then turned to Seikei. "They'll show you the way from here. Remember, at a tea ceremony, you must act the way a guest would normally do. No matter who else is present." Bunzo glanced at him. "Whoever that person might be. Do you understand?"

"Yes," said Seikei.

"Watch the judge and do whatever he does if you are uncertain," said Bunzo.

Seikei was bewildered. Clearly, he wasn't going to be punished, but he was awed by the fact that he would be allowed inside the shogun's palace. If only his father could see him now, he thought.

He had little time to think about it, for two of the guards motioned for him to cross the bridge across the moat and follow them. Inside, stone-covered paths led in all directions and Seikei saw dozens of the shogun's officials hurrying from one of the many buildings to another.

The guards led him toward the center of the huge

complex, and Seikei gazed with awe on the mighty fortress that was the home of the shogun. That was not their destination, however. One of the paths wound through a high hedge of yew bushes. On the other side was a stone garden like the one Seikei had seen at the judge's house. They walked around it, heading toward a small hut with a thatched roof at the far end.

As he came closer, Seikei saw that the hut was constructed of wooden beams that looked very old. Wormholes and cracks covered the wood, and crumbling dried clay filled the gaps between the beams. On this side, the hut had two small windows, but both were covered with wax paper so that no one could see in or out.

The entrance to the hut was a small opening, only as high as Seikei's waist. One of the guards pointed to it, and Seikei quickly removed his sandals, setting them beside two other pairs next to the doorway. He glanced at the guards, and they nodded. Seikei was to go in alone.

He stooped low, remembering that one must crawl through the doorway on hands and knees. This part of the tea ceremony was intended to humble everyone who went inside, another reminder that ranks were set aside. Within, even a merchant's son was the equal of anyone he encountered.

Inside, two men knelt on the bare wooden floor, sitting back on their heels. One was Judge Ooka, and the other . . . Seikei recognized him from the night before. Though the man was now dressed in a plain, undecorated kimono, it was he who had given the signal for the samurai to strike off Tomomi's head.

Seikei realized that he was in the presence of the shogun. He was relieved to see Judge Ooka smile reassuringly. Seikei knelt as the others had, and lowered his eyes shyly. He stared into the hot coals that glowed in a small pit in the center of the hut. A stick of incense and some pine needles had been placed within the pit to sweeten the smell of the smoke. A teakettle rested on a small grill over the coals.

"Here is the fine young man who has been so helpful," he heard the judge say.

"Welcome," said the shogun. "The water is almost boiling. I hope you will enjoy the tea."

It was impolite not to answer, and Seikei forced himself to look up. "I am sure that it will be a pleasant occasion," he replied, using one of the phrases he remembered from the ritual.

The shogun smiled. He was a heavy-set man about forty years old, the same age as Seikei's father. His face was soft and jowly, and when he smiled, tiny wrinkles appeared under his eyes. In fact, Seikei thought, he looked much like the merchants in Osaka who were his father's friends. Seikei reminded himself not to speak such a thought aloud.

All the utensils for the tea ceremony were set neatly beside the shogun. He picked up the bowl in which the tea would be brewed. At first glance, it appeared to be a simple bowl made of glazed clay. But Seikei saw that the glaze had been applied to make the bowl resemble a natural object, like something found in the forest by a hermit. The shogun poured a little hot water into it, swirled it around, and then discarded the liquid.

Now he opened a shiny lacquer box, and the scent of tea wafted into the room. Using a bamboo dipper, the shogun scooped some of the dark green powder into the purified bowl. By now, the water in the pot over the fire was bubbling softly, and the shogun gently added some to the bowl, stirring it with a whisk. As the powdered tea dissolved, the water turned into a thick, soupy liquid. When the brew was ready, the shogun handed the cup to Judge Ooka, who bowed his head in thanks, took three sips, and complimented the shogun on its taste.

Then he wiped the edge of the cup with a napkin and handed it to Seikei. Seikei accepted the bowl with both hands. Raising the bowl to his lips, Seikei discovered that the drink was smooth and full of subtle flavors. It was not mere politeness that caused him to take a second sip, and then a third.

"This is a very rare tea," he exclaimed. "It must have been grown on the western slopes of Mount Fuji, near Shizuoka." Remembering himself, he returned the cup to the shogun. "I thank you for allowing me to share such an excellent tea," Seikei said.

He noticed that both of the men were looking at him with interest. "I am pleased that you enjoyed the tea," said the shogun. He paused. "May I ask how you were able to identify the place where it was grown?"

Seikei's face grew hot. "I have tasted it before. My father has many different kinds of tea . . . in his store."

The shogun's eyes widened, and then he broke into a smile. Looking at Judge Ooka, he said, "Another of your surprises, my old friend."

"This young man has many talents," the judge replied. "I commend him highly."

The shogun looked at Seikei, who was trying not to show how much pride he felt in the judge's words. "As you know," the shogun said, "a tea ceremony is intended to give relief from everyday cares. Guests usually discuss such things as the tea, art, the beauty of nature."

Seikei nodded. Those were the things his father's friends spoke of at the ceremony he had attended. He had had to struggle not to let his boredom show.

"However," the shogun went on, "I always find it most enjoyable to hear how my friend Judge Ooka has solved a crime. In this case, I would particularly like to know how he contrived to bring the criminal before me to confess his crime and then demand his execution." He looked sternly at the judge, who bowed his head to conceal a smile.

The shogun looked back at Seikei. "Since you were involved in this matter, he thought you would enjoy it as well. But of course if you do not wish to hear about such a disturbing affair, it would not be polite to discuss it."

Seikei's mouth dropped. "Oh, no. I mean . . . that would give me great pleasure."

The shogun nodded and offered Seikei a tray of sweet little rice and bean cakes. Seikei took one and passed the tray to the judge, who said, "You will probably want more than one. Keep the tray, for I am already too fat." Then he reached out and murmured, "Perhaps just one, for the sake of politeness."

Seikei took a bite of his cake. "It has a delicious taste," he remembered to say. He looked over to see that the judge's cake had already disappeared. The shogun offered the judge another, but he shook his head firmly. "It is time to examine the path that we followed."

The End of the Path

"Truthfully," the judge began, "Seikei's alertness provided me with all the information I needed. When the jewel was stolen, it was apparent that the thief could not have been the paper-maker and his daughter, in whose room it was found. Surely they would have expected to be searched and would have tried to escape before morning came."

The judge looked at Seikei. "You were brave enough to admit that you had seen a spirit during the night. That was unusual enough to cause me to investigate. The jewel might have been stolen by a spirit, but I have yet to find even one case in which that was the solution." He shrugged. "Of course, life holds many strange things. But a spirit would not need to escape through a tunnel. So I advised you to follow it."

"But you were at the other end when I came out," Seikei recalled.

"Yes. I had heard that a kabuki troupe had performed nearby that evening. I thought that perhaps what you saw in the hallway of the inn might have been an actor, dressed in a costume.

"As you followed the tunnel, I walked to the temple grounds where the play had been performed. Of course, if you had come out in some other place, that would have told me that I was wrong."

"You were right," nodded Seikei. "It was Tomomi, dressed as a woman."

"If one of Lord Hakuseki's guards had been as alert as you, Tomomi would merely have posed as a geisha come to serve the daimyo." The judge paused for a sip of tea.

"I now knew how the crime had been committed," he continued. "However, the discovery of the tunnel showed me that the innkeeper was also suspect. For the kabuki actors could not have dug the tunnel. That required much time and work, and the innkeeper would surely have noticed such activity. So I ordered him arrested."

Seikei remembered the night of the bon festival when he had feared the spirit of the innkeeper. "But he killed himself under torture."

"Torture?" The judge shook his head. "No, I do not use torture. The shogun and I have discussed this before."

"And disagreed," grumbled the shogun.

"My feeling is that torture is useless in solving crimes," Judge Ooka said. "Most people will confess to anything if they are tortured long enough, whether they have committed a crime or not. My assistants merely show suspects the instruments of torture. In this case, the innkeeper was left alone with them, and he used a sword to commit seppuku. That showed me how unusual a crime this was. It told me all I needed to know."

"I remember your telling me that it meant he was a samurai," Seikei said.

The judge nodded. "A samurai who was willing to give up his own life to protect the man he served. A samurai working as an innkeeper is quite unusual. Killing himself to protect a kabuki actor would have been unthinkable—unless the actor was his lord."

The judge's hand crept toward the plate of sweet cakes, and Seikei moved it so that he could take one. By now, the second bowl of tea was ready—a sweeter, lighter drink than the first one. The judge gratefully sipped it and passed the bowl to Seikei.

"So you and I pursued the path of the thief," the judge went on. "He seemed unlikely to abandon his disguise, and I decided that he would try to lose himself in the crowds at Ise. When I discovered that a kabuki troupe was presenting *The Forty-Seven Ronin*, my suspicions were aroused." He looked at Seikei.

"You have certainly noticed the similarity between that story and this case."

Seikei nodded. "To avenge their lord, the ronin assumed roles that make people think they had lost their honor. Just as Tomomi did. But all the time, he was planning . . ."

"His revenge," nodded the judge. "That came later. Seeing Tomomi on stage, I realized what a cunning figure he was, and I sensed that he would be wary of someone pursuing him. I am too old and fat for that role, so I left you to follow the path."

Seikei shifted his legs. He wanted to ask the judge why he couldn't have made the message a little clearer. But the judge smiled, as if he had read Seikei's thoughts. "Left on your own, I assumed you would be resourceful. And don't forget, Bunzo was following to keep you from harm. He had already informed me of your confrontation with Tomomi in the teahouse."

Seikei felt humiliated. The judge knew, then, how Tomomi had taken the sword from him. "The next morning, Tomomi placed the jewel at the shrine, asking me to tell you."

"He hoped that I would concentrate my efforts on recovering the jewel. But as you now know, it was merely another false jewel. He kept the real one, for all along he intended to present it to the shogun himself."

Judge Ooka looked at the shogun. "You see, it was

not through any cleverness on my part that you witnessed the end of the drama. That was intended by Tomomi, or should we call him by his real name? Takezaki Genji. He announced that name in response to a challenge by Seikei."

"You challenged him?" the shogun asked, surprised.

"He only had a play sword," confessed Seikei. "And I lost."

"But you obtained from him the information that allowed me to understand his motive," said the judge. "I knew that the Takezaki family had been Kirishitans, and that their neighbor Lord Hakuseki had slain them and taken their lands. Lord Hakuseki reported that all the members of the family were dead, but as we saw, he lied."

"A dishonorable man," growled the shogun. "You know, he didn't even have the courage to commit seppuku properly. One of my samurai had to help him along."

Seikei felt a shiver run down his spine. Of course, that had been what Tomomi intended. By forcing Lord Hakuseki to draw his sword in the shogun's presence, he had condemned him to death. "What happened to the other actors?" he said, wondering how he dared to ask.

The shogun glanced at him. "They're in prison. Should I have them executed?"

"Oh, no," Seikei said at once. "They didn't know anything about what Tomomi was planning."

"Hm. You're sure of that?"

"Yes. Do you remember when Tomomi drew his father's sword at the play? One of the actors, a boy named Kazuo, warned Lord Hakuseki that it was real."

"I don't recall. It was confusing," said the shogun. "You don't think they deserve to be executed?"

Seikei shook his head.

"Well, then," said the shogun, shrugging. "If you wish it, I'll have them released." He turned to Judge Ooka. "But you knew what Tomomi was planning. Why didn't you warn me?"

"He would not have admitted his guilt so openly unless you were present. Tomomi had to be permitted to follow his own path. My samurai Bunzo followed Seikei, which was the only way I could learn of Tomomi's movements. Two nights ago, as Bunzo watched, Tomomi went to Lord Hakuseki's palace, disguised again as a woman."

"Bunzo followed me?" exclaimed Seikei.

"Certainly. He would not have let you come to harm."

Seikei remembered that Tomomi had almost choked him to death near Lord Hakuseki's yashiki that night. But he fought back the urge to point that out to the judge.

"Tomomi seems to have met Lord Hakuseki, convincing him that the performance of a play would please the shogun, something that Lord Hakuseki wished."

"You could have told me then and saved all this trouble," said the shogun.

"But you would not have had the pleasure of seeing a criminal confess to his crime in such an unusual way," said the judge.

"Hm. Once was enough. Do not repeat it."

"You were pleased?" asked the judge.

"Oh yes, it was exciting." The shogun laughed. "Did you see how those officials of mine scrambled to get out of the way of the fighting? There really aren't many true samurai anymore."

"I hope I will not offend you if I say that Takezaki Genji was a true samurai."

The shogun stared at Judge Ooka. "If so, why did he force me to consent to his execution? Why didn't he commit seppuku after drawing his sword in my presence?"

"I have decided," replied the judge, "that it was because he was a Kirishitan. Kirishitans do not commit seppuku."

Seikei spoke up. "Tomomi's mother committed seppuku, in the play."

The judge smiled. "An intelligent comment. But she had not been a Kirishitan before she married

Lord Takezaki. In the end, her samurai honor was stronger than the religion she adopted to please her husband. But her son . . ." He spread his hands.

"You see how dangerous these Kirishitan ideas are?" said the shogun. "If they were allowed to spread in Japan, then the samurai traditions would decay."

"I hoped you would mention that," said the judge. "For I have a favor to ask."

The shogun looked at him suspiciously. "I will not ban torture," he said. "Other judges are not so clever as you, and cannot do without it. If people didn't fear being punished for wrongdoing, the country would be filled with thieves."

"Not that," said the judge. "I know someone who is devoted to the ideal of bushido. He has shown himself to be courageous, honorable, and loyal. In every way, he is a true samurai."

"Name him," said the shogun. "I will make him a judge. Better yet, send him to my court to be an official, for I need such men."

"There is only one problem," said the judge. "He is not a samurai, but the son of a merchant."

Slowly, the shogun's eyes moved to Seikei. "You said your father sells tea?"

"And other things," said Seikei.

"Don't tell me about them," the shogun said with a wave of his hand. "I have too much to think about." He looked at the judge. "Someday you will test my patience too far," he said. "I suppose you have thought of some way to make this possible."

"Without violating tradition," the judge replied. "As you know, it is common for families without a son to adopt one to carry on their name. I have no son. If you consent, and if the father of this young man agrees, I will adopt him."

Seikei could not believe what he was hearing. The shogun looked him over slowly. "You wish this?" he said.

"Oh yes," said Seikei. "All my life I have wished to be a samurai."

"What about your own family? Have you not an obligation to them?"

Seikei considered. "My father has always said I have no head for business. In fact, he would be happier if Hachi, my younger brother, could take my place." He hesitated, thinking of his mother. She would miss him.

"Would I be able to visit my family?" he asked Judge Ooka.

The judge smiled. "I would not have it any other way." Then he turned to the shogun. "Well, my friend, what do you say?"

"Hm," said the shogun, eyeing Seikei. "Perhaps your father would make me a gift of tea?"

Seikei nodded, not daring to mention that his father's shop had some tea that was even better than the kind that the shogun had served.

"Make sure that your actions do not disgrace me," said the shogun. "I consent."

Seikei lowered his head, hiding his tears of joy.

"I see there are some of those cakes left," said the judge. "I think I'll have another."

Authors' Note

Judge Ooka was a real person, a friend and advisor of Yoshimune, the eighth shogun of the Tokugawa family. Yoshimune served as shogun between 1717 and 1744, and was eager to revive the samurai tradition and spirit. The story of "The Forty-Seven Ronin" is also a true one, which has inspired many Japanese playwrights and storytellers.

Judge Ooka did in fact oppose torture as a way of forcing a confession from suspects. The judge's ability to solve crimes through his amazing powers of reasoning made him famous even during his lifetime. Since then, tales about Judge Ooka have remained popular, causing some to call him the Sherlock Holmes of Japan. This story, however, comes from the imagination of the authors.